MW01244433

Real Life Romance

"EMPTY-NEST DOESN'T HAVE TO EQUAL LONELY-NEST.
CAN THEY FIND THE SPARK AGAIN?"

TARA CONRAD

His One Her Only Publishing

Contents

To my husband~ You're my moon and stars. My best friend. My soulmate.
My Real Life Romance.

1

Elizabeth

Today is a milestone day for Gilbert and me. It's the culmination of nearly two decades of planning. But to fully understand the significance, we need to take a little trip back in time.

All the way back to 1993, our senior year of high school.

It was Class Day. Do you remember that day? The one where all the prestigious senior awards like "Most Likely to Succeed" and "Most Likely to Cure Cancer" are handed out. Well, it came as no surprise to anyone when Gilbert Benton and Elizabeth Piazza were awarded "Couple Most Likely to Get Married."

And four months after graduation, we did just that.

Our wedding day was one of the best days of my life. When I close my eyes, the memory is still so vivid.

We didn't want anything big or fancy. So, we were thrilled when Gil's parents offered to host our wedding at their idyllic West Chester property. It was mid-October. The air was comfortable but still held that crisp scent belonging only to Autumn. The foliage was at its peak, adding pops of reds, yellows, and oranges as the perfect backdrop.

I wore an ivory long-sleeved bohemian style dress that was simple in design but made me feel like a princess. My long black hair hung in loose curls down my back. Gilbert wore tan linen pants and an ivory linen shirt. His reddish-brown hair was longer back then and blew in the breeze.

We said our vows under a rustic dark walnut arch that Gil built himself. His mother, Martha, artfully arranged white roses that trailed up the sides. It was exquisite. The arch with the now mature rose vines is still in their backyard. They've built a gazebo and enlarged the garden around it.

Then, after the sun had set and the air turned chilly, Gil and his best friend, who was also his best man, Chris, built a fire. A small gathering of our closest friends and family sat around the fire telling stories and singing songs until late in the night. It might not have been what many brides consider the ideal wedding, but for me, it exceeded every expectation.

That was twenty-seven years ago.

From that moment on, our lives have been planned out down to the second.

We wanted to have children, four to be precise. They were to be spaced evenly at two years apart. And we wanted to be young when we had them. So, while we were honeymooning, we also started practicing the age-old art of baby-making.

Fortunately for us, we had a knack for it, and nine months later, our first baby was born—a son, who we named Marco after my father. We were elated, totally head-over-heels for our red-haired, blue-eyed little boy.

Parenting was a breeze, so when Hunter came along, we were prepared—or so we thought. It quickly became clear that being the parents of a toddler and an infant was no joke. We were humbled very quickly as we stumbled through the balancing act of having two children. But even still, right on schedule, we had baby number three. A little girl we named Francesca. This time, we had a better idea of the chaos that would ensue once we arrived home with an infant, and the kids didn't disappoint. Then, right on schedule, baby number four—our little Grace arrived. Things couldn't have turned out any more perfect—two boys and two girls.

At twenty-six years old, we were done having babies and could now sit back and enjoy raising our family.

But having a family meant that our blissful newlywed days with lazy afternoons in bed and date nights every weekend became a thing of the past. Instead, they were replaced with four little people that now ruled our lives. Our days were filled with never-ending bottles, naps, laundry, and diapers. At one point, we had three children in diapers. Then came potty training and play dates—the list goes on and on.

Once the kids started hitting school age, things got even more interesting. Gil and I decided that instead of sending our children to school, we would homeschool instead. Our dining room was transformed into a one-room schoolhouse complete with ABC posters, maps, pencils, crayons, books, and years' worth of science projects.

Oh, those days were so hectic. Most days, even before Gil's alarm would go off, the pitter-patter of eight tiny feet would wake us up as they came bounding into our bedroom. Gil and I would pretend we were still asleep. The kids would be whispering and giggling quietly right before they pounced on the bed. Then Gil and I would implement our surprise tickle attack. I don't know who laughed more, us or the kids.

Each morning, we'd have breakfast as a family. Gil would say his goodbyes to each of us and then leave for work. We'd clean up the kitchen and move to the dining room, where we'd get set up for our school day.

Living in Philadelphia provided us with a unique opportunity to spend time at places like Independence Hall and the Franklin Institute. We believed in allowing the kid's curiosity to drive what we'd study and to do as much hands-on learning as we could. As a result, each child had the freedom to develop their individual passions. They also learned to support and respect the subjects their siblings loved.

But not a day went by that Gil didn't acknowledge that as a stay-at-home parent, I worked just as hard, if not harder, than he did. Most days, we maintained a great balance, but I can't lie, sometimes I felt utterly overwhelmed. Don't get me wrong, I loved every minute of it—well, maybe not every minute. There were plenty of days I would've given anything to trade places with Gil. The idea of getting dressed in professional clothes, leaving the house, and spending my day with other adults sounded very appealing.

Without the full support of my husband, I wouldn't have been successful in homeschooling. We complimented each other perfectly. Where I was spontaneous and free-spirited, Gil was regimented and organized. Gil handled the filing of the kid's schoolwork, making sure everything was in perfect order. At the end of the school year, when it came time to assemble their portfolios for the school district, I didn't have to do anything but put the pages in a binder.

He also kept a color-coded board that hung on our wall. Each of the kids had a color that corresponded with their activities. His efforts ensured we were always in the right place at the right time. Another bonus point for him—he cooked dinner every night. His children and I adored him. Still do.

Our home was a happy home, one where the kids always felt comfortable bringing their friends. Friday nights were movie nights. We'd make popcorn or have ice cream sundaes, and then we'd pile on the bean bag chairs and settle in for a movie. Saturday night was game night. It started as simple games like Candy Land and, as the children grew, progressed to strategic games like Risk. Every night we gathered at the table for family dinners where there was never a lack of conversation.

Then, one by one, our kids did exactly what we raised them to. They grew up and moved out to start lives of their own. It's been an exciting ride to watch them develop into successful twenty-somethings.

With Grace's homeschool graduation, our parenting days thankfully came to a close.

Fast forward back to today and why it's such a milestone. Today, our youngest child, the last stronghold, is moving out. Much to her father's dismay, she decided to attend the University of Hawaii to study marine biology.

We're currently on our way to the Philadelphia International Airport to put Grace on a plane so she can start living her dream.

"Are you certain you don't want to go with Rutgers?" Gil asks Grace for the thousandth time.

"I'm sure, dad."

"It's a much more sensible choice." He glances at her in the rearview.

"Dad." Grace leans forward. "We've talked about this. This is what I really want, and you promised you wouldn't give me a hard time today."

"I know. Hawaii is just so far away." Gil's voice cracks.

"I'm only an airplane ride away, daddy."

Gil parks the car and grabs the luggage. He drags his feet, trying to make the most of every last second we have with Grace. Finally, we arrive at the security checkpoint. It's as far as we can go with her. After a tearful goodbye, we stand arm-in-arm as we watch her walk away.

I'm a mix of so many emotions. Pride. Fear. But most of all, excitement for what Grace's future holds.

On our way home from the airport, we stop at our favorite restaurant, Morimoto. Gil called ahead to reserve us a quiet table in the corner. Not only did he have a stunning bouquet of red roses waiting for me at our table, but he also pre-arranged our menu. It was a very romantic evening that continued long after we got home.

At only forty-six years old, we're officially empty nesters. We've successfully checked off all the boxes on our to-do list and are ready to begin the next phase of our life.

2

Gilbert

Today's the day I've been both looking forward to and dreading at the same time. It's the day that Grace, my baby girl, is leaving me and moving halfway across the world to attend the University of Hawaii.

Growing up, Grace became passionate about marine biology. We were fortunate enough to live close to the Adventure Aquarium, where we held a season pass. She took advantage of the aquarium's many educational programs and even worked there part-time while she was in high school. So, it came as no surprise when she applied to colleges that had Marine Biology programs. She was not only accepted to every school she applied to, she also received scholarships to several, including Rutgers University and the University of Hawaii—her final two choices.

Of course, I strongly encouraged her to go to Rutgers. It's a well-respected university, and it's within driving distance. Both were a win for me because she could still come home on weekends. But no, my headstrong daughter insisted on the University of Hawaii.

Today's the big day—the day I've been dreading.

The airport is bustling with travelers going to and from their intended destinations. Grace buzzes with excitement while we walk to the gate for her flight. I, however, am now enjoying this. We take her as far as we can—the security checkpoint. She and her mom embrace in a tearful hug before Grace turns to me.

"I'm so proud of you, Gracie-girl." I wrap my arms around my daughter and hold her tight, not ready to let go. "It's not too late to change your mind."

She ignores my comment.

"I love you, Daddy." Grace wipes her eyes. "I promise I'll call every weekend."

"You can call more than just once a week." I kiss her forehead.

"I'll try." She looks over her shoulder. "Time for me to go."

And with that, Grace turns around and walks toward the security checkpoint.

My daughter is all grown. Although she's the picture of confidence and maturity, all I see is my little girl running in the park, her dark chestnut pigtails bouncing behind her. Her contagious laughter filling the air.

Liz slides her arms around my waist.

"She'll do terrific."

I nod and put my arm around my wife. She rests her head on my chest.

We stay until Grace clears security and is out of sight.

Grace has held true to her word and video calls us every Saturday afternoon. She loves her classes and seems like she's adjusted to living on the island quite easily.

Now, it's officially just Lizzie and me.

Twenty-seven blissful years. That's how long Lizzie and I have been married. My high school sweetheart has grown up by my side. Not a day has gone by that she hasn't taken my breath away just by being herself.

Having children right after we got married wasn't easy. It meant giving up those precious first few years when most newlyweds are adjusting to being married, traveling, and basically just spending time together—alone. Lizzie and I made a plan to do things differently.

Instead of waiting, we had our children young and in quick succession. It was important to me that our children be no more than two years apart. Why would that be so important? Because I have a brother, Ryan, who is eight years younger than me.

I'll never forget the day my parents sat me down and told me I was going to be a big brother, that my mom was going to have a baby. I didn't believe them. I was sure it was some sort of joke. Even as my mom's stomach grew bigger, my eight-year-old brain convinced itself she was just gaining weight. It made perfect sense to me.

Then, one day I woke up, and instead of my mom being downstairs, my grandparents were at my house to babysit me. They told me mom was in the hospital and would have a surprise for me. When they came home a few days later, with my supposed surprise, I was shocked. In my mom's arms was a tiny baby—my brother. That's when I realized they'd been telling me the truth all along—and I didn't like it one bit.

Everything about our lives changed the day they brought baby Ryan home. My routine life was turned upside-down, and it never returned to my comfortable and safe norm. The harder my parents tried to get me to bond with the baby, the more I grew to resent him. The baby turned into a toddler who was always into my things. Then, the toddler turned into an even more annoying child who wanted to tag along with my teenage friends and me. As adults, we don't call or hang out with each other. We never bonded as siblings, and now we have nothing in common. We're brothers, but we're not friends.

That's something I wanted to avoid with my children.

Since Lizzie and I knew we wanted more than one child and it was important to me that my children never experienced what I did, we agreed having four children spaced two years apart would be perfect. The age span would allow us to have time to bond with a new baby and would still ensure the kids would be close growing up. It was important to me that we provide the framework for them to be not only siblings but also friends. And that strategy seemed to work well.

Throughout the years, my Lizzie has been the picture of strength as she grew round carrying each of our children and giving birth to them. As a parent, she was patient with her guidance and correction. As their teacher, she allowed them freedom to be curious and explore, which led them to love learning.

And as a wife, she's always been loving and attentive. My friends questioned my sanity when I first told them we were getting married right after high school, but not a day went by that I ever questioned or doubted my decision. I always believed if I were able to rewind time, I'd do everything the same way. But lately, I've been questioning our decisions.

We had a plan for this time in our lives. It was supposed to be perfect. Without the demands of raising children, we'd be able to focus on each other. We could eat out every night if we wanted and we could travel. The world was our oyster. But that isn't the reality I'm living.

Lizzie seems to have adjusted to being an empty nester. She's never had trouble with a change in routine. Rather, she embraces it with open arms. Just like she's doing with our newfound freedom. On the other hand, I'm paralyzed by fear of the unknown.

For years, when I came home from work, I knew just what to expect. The kids would be waiting for me to do schoolwork with them or show me what projects they did during the day. Even as they grew older, I knew there would always be a job for 'Dad' when I got home.

But now, I come home from work, and I don't know what to do with myself. No kids are waiting for me. Lizzie has the housework done and dinner on the stove. Our family's routine that was so comfortable for me has been obliterated.

I'm jealous of my wife's ability to smoothly transition into this new life while I'm struggling to figure out where I fit, which leaves me terrified.

What if all our plans were for nothing? What if Lizzie wakes up and realizes my dependence on structure and routine isn't okay anymore? That I'm no longer who she wants.

3

Elizabeth

Chapter Three- Elizabeth

Beep. Beep. Beep. Gil's clock radio, the same one he's had since high school, wakes us up at six a.m. At this point, his body operates on pure muscle memory as he reaches his hand over and turns off the alarm. It's the same routine we've had for so many years.

Grace has been gone for almost two months now, and instead of living it up and having fun, it's one monotonous day after another. Today, I'm going to try to change that.

Rolling over, I prop myself on my elbow. "How about you call off today? We can spend the day doing something fun."

"I can't do that."

"Why not?"

"I have to inspect a new apartment building in Brewerytown," Gil explains.

"You run the department. Can't you have someone else do it?

After we got married, Gil not only worked full-time, he also went to college and earned his bachelor's degree in business and a master's degree in public administration. He's passionate about bringing affordable, safe housing to the citizens of Philadelphia and has worked his way up in the housing authority. Several years ago, he was promoted to Executive Director. I'm so proud of his achievements. He's always been a hard worker and has done a great job providing for our family. The one area he struggles with is delegating responsibilities and using the ample amount of vacation, and personal time he's allotted.

"No. I'm the one scheduled to do it." He climbs out of bed.

"Oh." I flop back onto the pillow.

I watch as Gil goes about his daily routine. Despite my disappointment, I smile because he never deviates from the pattern. First, he takes off his pajamas, shirt, and then pants which fall into a pile outside of the laundry basket. Next, he puts on a pair of boxers followed by dark blue jeans and his uniform shirt. Right foot first, he puts on his sock and shoe before switching feet and doing the same. Then, he heads downstairs. That's my cue to get up and make the coffee while Gil makes breakfast.

We're officially stuck in a rut.

After he leaves for work, I get the housework done and head to my office to type up this week's blog.

Back when our oldest was just starting middle school, I didn't know of any other homeschooling families. I felt alone—isolated. And the kids weren't feeling much better. So, I decided if I couldn't find an already established homeschooling group, I'd start one.

I got in touch with the librarian at our closest branch, and together we started a group for local homeschooling families. We'd meet once a month and teach a group activity, and we also had a book club. Our kids got a chance to socialize, and so did the parents. It was the boost I needed to keep going.

That's how I got started with my blog, "Finding my Tribe." It was my way of reaching out, albeit virtually, to other homeschooling moms who might be feeling the way I did before I found my local tribe. Homeschooling isn't for the faint of heart, and if there was any way I could be a support to another parent, I was all in.

At first, I only had a few pity followers being our parents and my best friend, Kelly. But as time moved on and I posted more, my audience grew. A year in, I had a couple thousand followers. What started as a place to talk about homeschooling has become so much more. These people, some of whom I've met in person, have become my second family. We've been together through many life events births of children, graduation of our high schoolers, and deaths of loved ones. I think it's time I take my concerns to them and get some advice because I'm out of ideas.

I open the webpage and write an entry.

Have you ever found yourself repeating a pattern you thought you couldn't get out of? Well, tribemates, that's precisely where I'm finding myself right now. You all know our youngest left for college two months ago. Btw, she's absolutely loving school and Hawaii! You also know how excited I was to be an empty nester. Well, things aren't working out quite as planned. Maybe that's the issue. This was supposed to be the time Gil and I did things unplanned, spontaneous, on a whim—whatever you'd like to call it. There's a big problem with that. Gil is not a 'fly by the seat of your pant's kinda guy. He thrives on organization and routine. He's still trying to live by our old routine, which doesn't work anymore. He's reluctant to let go and try something new. Gil and I have never been on different pages like this, and I don't know what to do? How do I get him to turn the page and join me in this next chapter?

This is supposed to be an exciting time for us, but...

We're stuck in a rut—a very deep rut!

~Lizzie

4

Gilbert

Grace wasn't able to make it home for Thanksgiving. She said her school break wasn't long enough to fly back and forth. I didn't like not having her here, but I knew the semester would be over soon, and she'd be home for a few weeks over Christmas.

I'm very much looking forward to the holidays and have it all planned out. We'll visit the Christmas Village in Love Park, like we do every year, to pick our family ornament. One evening we'll go ice skating at the RiverRink. Another night, we'll go see the lights at Miracle on South 13th Street—that's been a favorite of the kids since they were little. And we'll take an evening to decorate the tree. With all four of the kids home, it'll be perfect.

With a spreadsheet open in front of me, I send out a group text to find out when each of them will be arriving. Preparedness and organization are the key.

(Dad) Hoping to get an idea when to expect each of you home for Christmas. I have a lot of fun family activities planned.

It takes a few minutes for their replies to start flooding in. And when they do, they aren't the replies I'm expecting.

(Hunter) I was going to call you this weekend. The guys and I booked an Airbnb in Florida. We're spending the holiday on the beach.

(Francesca) Ryker and I will be there for Christmas Eve. We're going to spend Christmas with his family.

(Dad) What about the week before, you always stay at home, Frannie?

(Francesca) Neither of us could get the week off. Sorry, Dad.

My pulse skyrockets, and I break out in a cold sweat. Relax, Gil; all is not lost. There're still two kids who'll be here.

(Marco) Um…Ivy's parents invited us to spend the holiday with them at their vacation house in the Pocono's. I was going to let you know when I came over tomorrow.

Ivy is Marco's fiancé, they're getting married next year. They always spend the holiday here. Now they won't be here at all?

I click the little x to close my spreadsheet. There's no reason to have it. Brick by brick, the kids are demolishing my plans.

(Dad) Grace, you're still coming home, right?

I see she's read the text, but she doesn't respond. A few minutes later, my phone rings.

"Hi, daddy." Grace's cheery voice is like a balm to my soul.

"How's my baby girl doing?"

"I'm good. How's mom?"

"She's keeping busy."

There's a long, awkward pause. Something tells me this isn't a call to give me her flight information, but I ask anyway.

"What day will you be flying home?"

"Well, um…I'm not going to be able to come home for Christmas."My stomach turns.

"What do you mean you aren't coming home for Christmas?"

"The conservation center needed volunteers for the holidays since the animals still require care. So, I volunteered to stay."I'm silent as I count to ten and take deep breaths—whatever I need to do so I don't lose my mind completely.

"Dad?" Grace asks. "Are you still there?"

"I'm here."

"You're not upset, right?"

Upset? Why would I be upset? Just because all the plans I made are now ruined.

"No, not at all."

"Oh good, I was afraid you'd be mad."

Grace changes the subject and tells me all about the friends she's made and the work she's doing at the conservatory. When we hang up, I drop my head in my hands.

In under an hour, everything I'd planned for the holiday has been ruined.

This is the first Christmas Lizzie, and I have spent alone since the year we were married.

"We can still do everything you planned," Lizzie says as she wraps garland around the wood handrail on our staircase. "It'll be fun."

"Yeah, I guess so."

"You guess so?" She puts her hands on her waist. "You're making me feel like you don't want to spend time alone with me."

"That's not it. It's just that we've always done these things with the kids."

"And now." She walks over to me and puts her arms around my neck. "We can do it together."

"Yes, we can." I manage a smile.

It's not that I don't want to be alone with Liz. I do. But there's this emptiness inside that I don't know what to do with.

We spend the rest of the evening decorating the house. Lizzie isn't satisfied until every last string of garland and wreath is in place.

"Let's go outside and see how the lights look." She slips her shoes on and wraps a blanket around her shoulders, and we go outside.

I click the button on the remote, and the house lights up. The roof is trimmed in strings of transparent lights, and each window has a candle with a light that flickers like a real flame. It's a simple yet elegant design.

"Beautiful, as always." I compliment my wife's efforts.

The air is cold, and she snuggles close to me. "Since it'll be just the two of us, I was thinking maybe we could go out to eat for Christmas."

"We always make ravioli."

Lizzie's family is Italian, and even though cooking isn't something she typically enjoys, she goes all out for the holidays. When her Nonna was alive, everyone would gather at her house, where they'd make hundreds of homemade ravioli. After she passed, Lizzie and her mom, Carmela, continued that tradition with our kids. I assumed we'd keep that the same this year.

"I know we do, but I thought we could try something different," she says as we walk into the house.

"I don't know."

I head straight to the couch and flop down. Lizzie lays down and puts her head in my lap.

At the mere thought of any more changes, tension begins coiling in my toes and makes its way up my body. The day-to-day changes we've gone through have been bad enough. With the house empty, the nonstop chatter of our kids trying to tell us everything important about their day is gone. Now, it's just Liz and me. We don't have family movie nights on Friday, and even though we've kept Saturday game day, it's not as exciting with only two players.

And now our holiday traditions are in danger of changing too.

"Give it some thought." She teases my thigh with her finger. "Making new traditions for the two of us could be fun."

"I'd rather keep things the same."

Lizzie sighs loudly and sits up.

"Gil, you need to take a deep breath and at least try to go with the flow." And with that, she walks away, leaving me sitting in the living room staring at the twinkling lights of our Christmas tree.

If only she knew how much I'd love to go with the flow, but I'm not wired that way.

Even as our kids became teenagers, when the sun rose on Christmas day, they'd turn into five-year-olds again. The same young adults who'd sleep until late in the afternoon any other day of the year would be up at the crack of dawn banging on our bedroom door to wake us up because, well, presents.

But not this Christmas.

This Christmas it's Lizzie and me who sleep in. It's nearing one p.m. before we crawl out of bed and grab some coffee before making our way to the living room. We exchange the few gifts we bought one another and then, just like that, it's over. I want to be happy and enjoy the day, but the stack of unopened gifts in the corner and the hole in my heart remind me of everything that's missing.

Later in the afternoon, we have a video call with all the kids. They're excited to show us the gifts they opened.

"Check it out," Marco says and turns the camera so we can see out the window. "We got a foot of snow overnight."

"It's snowing here now," Francesca adds. "Is it snowing in Philly?"

"There's a few flurries, but nothing that's accumulated," Liz says. "I wish we were snowed in. That would be so much fun."

"I'll take this view any day of the week," Hunter says and turns his camera to show us the beach view from where he's sitting.

"Mine is even better," Grace says and shows us the dolphin she's in the middle of feeding.

"Fine, you win, Grace," Hunter jokes.

For over an hour, I get the illusion that we're all together, but then the kids say their goodbyes. My illusion breaks into tiny pixels, and I'm back to sulking on the couch.

Things pick up again for the early evening. Both sets of our parents come over for a ravioli dinner—finally something familiar. I'm prepared for the grandparents to be sullen without their grandkids here, but they don't appear fazed by their absence. It becomes clear that I'm the only one struggling today.

Dinner is delicious as usual. Afterward, the men and women split up. The women congregate in the kitchen to clean up, and the men take their coffees to the living room. Lizzie's one rule on Christmas is no TV watching, so my father, father-in-law, and I are stuck sitting and listening to the Christmas songs on one of the television holiday music stations.

"Are you and Lizzie enjoying newlywed life again, son?" Dad asks.

"We're still trying to adjust to all the changes." This is my chance to get some back-up on my feelings. "How did you and mom get along after Ryan and I were out of the house? I'm sure it was hard being alone."

"We took advantage of every second." Dad chuckles. "I don't think you really want me to elaborate on that, though."

He's right. I don't want to hear about what he and mom get up to in their alone time. I may be a grown man, but that's still TMI.

No dice with my parents, but Liz's parents must've had a hard time. With her being an only child, their lives revolved around her. She was there one day and moved out the next. I'm certain they'll understand my dilemma.

"What about you, Marco? Did you and Carmela have a difficult transition after Lizzie moved out?

"It was an adjustment. Carmela struggled the most," he says and then looks adoringly at his wife, who's in the kitchen drying dishes. "It took a few months for us to find a new groove, but once we did, it was smooth sailing."

"Liz seems to be handling everything okay. I'm assuming it's you struggling. You never were one for change," Dad says.

"I'll be honest. I'm not liking it very much."

"That's understandable. You and Liz didn't have much time just to be a couple before you started having kids," Marco adds. "It's time to take advantage of that now, though. You two should take an extended vacation."

"I can't leave work for that long."

"Gilbert, the housing authority won't fall apart if you aren't there for a few weeks. Marco's right. I think a vacation would do you two some good." Dad smiles. "Call it a second honeymoon."

I thought I'd find more solidarity from our fathers. Lizzie was, still is, daddy's little girl. I was certain Marco was going to tell me how he got depressed when she left and how he wished she'd come home, but no, he's encouraging me to take a vacation. And my dad's backing him up.

Why am I the only one struggling with how different our lives are? Having our kids grown and moved out was a time we both looked forward to. When we'd get to do everything we'd always dreamed about. Instead, I find myself searching for the rewind button, but it's not there.

I'm beginning to think there's something wrong with me.

5

Elizabeth

Things aren't getting better. It feels like Gil and I are slipping farther away from each other. I know he's disappointed Grace didn't come home for Christmas. But she volunteered to stay and care for the animals over the holiday, and we've always taught our kids to honor their commitments. She can't just walk away from a promise.

We improvised and mailed each other gifts. It was a few days late, but we opened them together on a video call. It wasn't the same as always, but it was still fun.

I thought Gil would be happy when Hunter, Marco, Ivy, Francesca, and Ryker came for a surprise visit to ring in the New Year with us. And he was, momentarily. Once they left, he slipped back into sulking.

Gil thrives on patterns and routines. That's something I've always known and accepted. We've always found ways to make transitions go more smoothly for him. I'll admit, there's been a lot of changes. However, none of them have been a surprise. We knew our kids were growing up, that they'd eventually move out. It's part of parenting.

Gil and I have looked forward to what life would be like when the kids moved out. We'd be free to do whatever we wanted, when we wanted. I envisioned us being more romantic with each other. And that we'd travel and do all the other things we talked about doing. But none of that is happening.

I've been trying to be patient. To give Gil time and space to work through his feelings. Our lives are totally different now. I acknowledge that. I feel it too. It was me that was the stay-at-home parent—my entire life revolved around the kids. But I'm finding this part of motherhood, the part where I can sit back and watch them make their own path in life, to be even more satisfying.

I'm eager to move on and embrace this new chapter in our lives. But that's not the way things are turning out. I'm scared that this is more than him having the blues because the kids are moving on. I'm starting to think that maybe he doesn't want me anymore. I'm afraid to ask him, scared of what his answer will be.

I'm not sure what to do, so I text my best friend, Kelly. She and her husband, Brian, don't have kids, but she always knows what to do in any situation.

(Liz) Got a few minutes?

(Kelly) For you, always.

(Liz) I need some marriage advice.

(Kelly) Oh? What's going on?

(Liz) Can I call?

(Kelly) Of course

I get Kelly on the phone and fill her in on everything that's been going on and not going on between us. She listens quietly before giving her opinion.

"We all know Gil's a creature of habit," Kelly says, and we both laugh. "No matter how uncomfortable it might be for him, he's going to have to learn some new habits."

"I'd be happy if he seemed even to notice I'm in the same room."

I've never felt like this before. Gil and I have always been like two peas in a pod. We did everything together. He always made me feel like the center of his universe, but since Grace left, all he does is mope around feeling sorry for himself.

We're supposed to be free to be into each other. Instead, I feel like I'm invisible.

"When's the last time you two had sex?" Kelly asks.

"Umm..." It takes a minute to figure it out. "The night Grace left for Hawaii."

"Elizabeth," Kelly shrieks so loud I have to pull the phone away from my ear. "That's almost six months ago."

"I'm well aware of that fact." I roll my eyes.

"Get dressed. I'll be over to get you in twenty minutes."

"Where are we going?"

"Just get dressed and be ready to go."

I should've known Kelly would come in like a whirlwind.

After she picks me up, our first stop is for lunch at one of my favorite noodle restaurants. Our next stop is for mani and pedis and a full Brazilian wax. Then, I'm informed the stylist is ready to do my hair.

"This would look amazing on you." Kelly shows me a picture of a short, dramatically styled cut.

"Absolutely not," I argue.

"Come on, live a little," Kelly encourages. "If you hate it, it's just hair. It'll grow back."

I won't cave on this one. I love my long hair. After some back and forth, we agree on a healthy trim and some layers.

Now we're in a little boutique on South Street buying something sexy for tonight. Kelly keeps pulling out racy little numbers, but I shake my head to them all. They just aren't me. We settle on a silky black slip nightdress with spaghetti straps that hang to my mid-thigh.

"Are you sure this will look okay?" I hold it up over my clothes in front of the mirror.

"It'll look more than okay. You're going to look hot," Kelly says, a bit too loud for my liking. "This is sure to snap Gil out of his slump."

I stare at the piece of lingerie for a few more minutes, uncertain if I should buy it. My body doesn't look anything like it did when Gil and I first got married. Back then, I was young and very fit. My petite frame seemed to look fabulous in anything I put on, but I'm not eighteen anymore. I've had four babies, and it shows. Parts of me that used to be perky now droop. The toned abdomen I once had is still flabby and sports more stretch marks than unblemished skin. Although I work out regularly, my body doesn't look like I want it to. Maybe I should start going to the gym? I could get a personal trainer.

"Come on." Kelly grabs my arm. "Let's check out before you change your mind."

That evening I order from our favorite Japanese restaurant. The table is set with real dishes instead of our usual paper plates. Candles are lit and soft music is on to set the mood. We'll have a romantic dinner and then head upstairs, where we'll hopefully continue the romance.

The food arrived and is on warm in the oven. I expect Gil to be home any minute. Every time I hear a car, I run to the window, but it's not him. The minutes tick by, and still no Gil. I try his cell, and it goes to voicemail.

(Liz) Hey babe. Obviously, you're running late. Can you give me an ETA?

Usually, he reads my texts right away, but it's sitting unopened.

Another half-hour goes by, and this time, I call his office phone, something I try not to do unless it's an emergency.

The line rings several times before someone answers.

"Philadelphia Housing Authority, Camila speaking. How can I help you?"

Why is Camila in my husband's office answering his phone? I can't stand this woman.

Camila and I first met at last year's office Christmas party. She's only been at the office a little over a month, so I hadn't met her yet. From the second we were introduced, it was clear we weren't going to be besties. Camila gushed over what a terrific boss my husband was while she put her hand on his arm. She was way too familiar with him. Things only got worse as the night went on. Since then, I try to avoid her whenever possible.

"Hi Camila," I say in a saccharine sweet voice. "It's Elizabeth. Is Gil still there?"

"He's here, but he's busy at the moment."

"I'll wait."

"I don't know how long he'll be."

"Is Liam still there?"

"No. Everyone else went home."

"Can you tell him his wife called?"

"Of course. Have a good evening."

Camila quickly disconnects the phone.

All sorts of scenarios run through my head—none of them good.

Why is Gil at the office late, and only Camila is there? Is Gil having an affair? Is that why he's not interested in me when he's home? "Stop letting your mind go there, Elizabeth," I say to no one. I don't trust Camila, but Gil would never betray me like that. Right?

6

Gilbert

I step out of my office for two minutes to grab a file from the conference room when I hear Camila answering my phone.

"Who was that?" I ask. It's odd for the phone to ring after hours.

"It was a wrong number." She shrugs.

"Next time, let it ring. My voicemail will pick up."

Tonight's another late night, something that's been happening more frequently. Camila did a solo inspection earlier today and messed up all the permit paperwork. She's been here long enough that she shouldn't be making these kinds of mistakes. They take hours of work to correct. It would've been nice to let it wait until morning, but these are time-sensitive documents which mean staying to fix it all tonight—and Camila isn't getting off the hook. She needs to take responsibility for her mistakes, which means she stays late too.

I've just finished uploading everything into the city's database so we can finally go home.

"Thank you for helping fix my mess." Camila touches my arm. "I don't know why I can't seem to get the hang of this."

"Hopefully, it won't happen again."

I pick up my cell and see Lizzie texted me over an hour ago, but I didn't get the notification. That's odd. Then I see my volume is turned off. I always leave it on. I must've bumped the button during all this chaos.

(Gil) I just got your text. There was an emergency at the office. I'm on my way out now.

It's dark as we exit the building, and even though the neighborhood is relatively safe, I still walk Camila to her car.

"I'm going to stop for a bite to eat." She leans against her car door. "Any chance you'll join me. It's the least I can do for keeping you so late."

"Thanks, but I'm going to head home."

"Next time, then." She smiles and slides into the driver's seat.

As soon as she closes the door, I head to my minivan—destination home.

When I get home, I'm greeted by a dark house. That's odd. Lizzie always waits up for me.

"Liz, where are you?" I call as I turn on the light and walk through the house, but there's no answer.

When I walk into the dining room, there are candles that I can see were burning but have since been extinguished, and the table is set for two. Thrown over the back of Lizzie's chair is a silky black piece of lingerie. I venture into the kitchen, and sitting on the stove is cold hibachi and a tray of sushi. Liz went through a lot of trouble setting up a romantic evening for us.

"Gil, you really messed up this time."

Figuring she must be upstairs, I grab the lingerie and take the steps two at a time. Our bedroom door is shut. Although I'm afraid of what will happen when I open the door, I know I need to face the music. With great trepidation, I reach out and turn the handle and then push the door open.

Lizzie's wearing her favorite pajamas and is lying in bed reading a book. She doesn't even look up when I start walking toward her. Even when I sit on the bed next to her, I get no reaction. She just flips the page and keeps reading.

"I'm sorry."

"Mhm."

Uh oh. I'm only getting sounds instead of words. That means she's too mad to even yell at me.

"I'm sorry I didn't let you know I was going to be late. I had no idea you were planning a special evening."

She sets the book down and looks at me, her blue eyes a turbulent swirl of anger.

"I guess you were too busy with Camila to think about me."

"What are you talking about?"

"I called your office, Gil," she says. "Camila answered and told me how busy you were."

What does she mean she called the office? The phone only rang one time. Camila said it was a wrong number, though.

"Lizzie," I put my hand on her arm. "I heard the phone ring, but I was in the other room grabbing a file. I'm sure that's all she meant."

"I don't think that's what she was alluding to." Liz's words are clipped.

"And what do you think she was trying to say?" I'm not sure where Liz is going with this.

"I think something's going on between you and Camila." She crosses her arms.

Is she for real right now? "The reason Camila was there is because she messed up paperwork on some important permits. They were time-sensitive, and I wasn't about to fix it myself. I made her stay to correct her mistakes." I pause. "Camila didn't tell me you called."

"I texted you too."

"I saw that right before I texted you. For some reason, my volume was turned down." I'm still not sure how that happened. I'll have to be more careful from now on. But right now, that's not important. What is important is Liz thinking something's going on between Camila and me. "How could you think I'd be interested in anyone but you?"

"Since Grace left, we don't talk anymore—you're distant. I feel like you don't want to spend time with me. And then, tonight, when you didn't call or answer my text, my imagination ran wild."

I drop my head because I know everything she's saying is the truth and that I'm responsible for her feeling abandoned. But I don't know how to tell her how I'm feeling. What my fears about us are. I'm afraid she'll look at me differently—not see me as a man.

"You're right, and I'm sorry. I'll take care of everything at the office. It won't happen again." I hold up the lingerie. "What's this?"

"It was supposed to be for tonight."

"I'd love to see you model it."

"Maybe another night," she says. "I'm really not feeling it anymore."

"I understand." I lean over and place a kiss on her cheek. "I'm sorry, Liz."

7

Elizabeth

Part of me is relieved when Gil explained why he was at the office and that it was nothing like the scenarios my overactive brain conjured up. But it did prove once more that Camila's sneaky. I'm convinced she's after my husband.

Speaking of my husband, what am I going to do about him? He's not been the same since we've become a childless household. He apologized, and I do forgive him, but I also know he's holding something back. It's obvious he's stuck in parenting mode. I don't know why, but he's having a hard time shifting into husband mode. He's missing all the fun we could be—should be having.

I was planning to seduce him tonight, but obviously, that didn't turn out as planned. It's time to take more drastic measures, but I'm out of ideas. While Gil is downstairs eating, I sneak into my office for a few minutes and fire up my laptop.

Good evening tribe. First, thank you for sharing your stories with me. As always, I appreciate your willingness to be open and honest. Overwhelmingly, what I heard was to be patient. That relearning life after the kids move out can be difficult for some people. I was also given the advice to do something special—something unexpected. Well, tonight, I tried that, and it was an epic fail. I'm frustrated, but I'm not giving up. I'm far too stubborn for that. Even worse. I think another woman is gunning for my man, and I need to put a stop to it. So, I plan to go bigger. I have an idea that hubby won't see coming but should knock him off his feet—and hopefully out of his pants.

I'm going to need your help with some more creative ideas on how to woo my husband! Can you all lend a hand? Send me everything you've got!!~Lizzie

I hit send. Now I have to wait for the responses to start coming in.

The following day, I place a call to Gil's secretary.

"Liam, how are you today?"

"Nothing to complain about. For today at least." He chuckles.

"I have a huge favor to ask."

"Anything for you."

"What does Gil's schedule look like tomorrow?"

"Let me check." Liam's keyboard clicks loudly. "He's in a meeting in the morning, other than that, nada. It looks like a light day."

"Can you book an appointment around lunchtime? Don't tell him it's me. Make it something he won't question but will keep him in his office."

"Sounds like someone is planning a surprise."

"I am. I'm feeling the need to make an appearance and stake my claim."

"Let me guess, Camila?"

I can hear Liam roll his eyes through the phone.

"How did you know?"

"She doesn't try to hide it. She walks around like she was hired to flirt with Mr. Benton.

I swear steam releases from my ears. How dare she think she can flirt with my husband?

"But don't worry." Liam interrupts my thoughts. "Mr. Benton doesn't reciprocate her advances. Actually, I don't even think he notices."

The reassurance that Gil isn't into Camila is helpful but knowing she's openly flirting with him only fuels my plan.

"Will Camila be there as well?"

"I'll make sure of it."

I smile, thankful that Liam is willing to be my co-conspirator in Operation Stake My Claim.

8

Elizabeth

My eeting with Gil is in a half-hour. I've flat ironed my hair, so it hangs silky smooth. My make-up is on par—smoky eyes and all. Next, I grab a sexy open-shouldered top and a pair of jeans, the ones Gil loves because of how they hug my curves. I finish the ensemble with a pair of black suede thigh-high boots with heels and then give a slow twirl in the mirror. It takes a lot of willpower to ignore the parts of my body I don't like, but overall, I'm happy with how I look today.

On my way out, I use a food delivery app to have lunch delivered to the office. When I step outside, my ride is waiting. I fidget nervously in the back seat as we drive across town. Although taking a risk usually doesn't bother me, this is so far out of my norm. I'm terrified my surprise visit will backfire and make things worse. My rising anxiety is proof of it.

When we're a few blocks away, I pull out my compact to double-check my make-up and apply the finishing touches—a deep red lipstick. I finish just as we pull up outside Gil's building.

My heels click on the tiled floor as I stride through the entrance hall to the elevators. It's a quick ride to the third floor. When the doors open, I step out into the reception area, where Liam sits behind his desk.

"You look hot today, Mrs. Benton."

I blush at his compliment.

"If I found a woman like you, I'd consider being straight." We both laugh.

"Is Gil in his office?"

"Yes, ma'am. He and Camila are waiting for his one o'clock."

"I'll take care of that." I smile and head straight to my husband's office at the end of the hall.

Since I'm going for the element of surprise, I don't bother to knock. Gil's head shoots up from his computer screen when I open the door. He looks like he's ready to reprimand whoever just barged into his office unannounced, but when he sees me, his jaw drops. Camila, who's sitting in a chair across from his desk, turns to see what Gil's looking at. What's even funnier is her jaw drops too.

"I wasn't expecting you." Gil stands and meets me halfway, giving me a kiss.

"That's the point." I look over his shoulder at Camila, who's now leaning against Gil's desk. Her eyes are narrowed as she watches us.

"Knock. Knock," Liam says from the doorway. "Lunch is here."

"Liz, I wish I had time. I have an appointment that'll be starting any minute."

"I know." I smile. "I'm your appointment."

Gil looks between Liam and me.

"I couldn't say no to the boss's wife." He hands Gil our bag of food.

"I ordered sandwiches from Yardan's Deli."

"My favorite."

Gil peeks in the bag to inspect the contents while I slip off my coat and drop it onto the chair Camila vacated.

"It's so nice to see you again, Camila." I acknowledge her presence briefly and then turn my attention back to my husband.

"Always a pleasure to see you too."

"It looks like I won't be needing you after all," Gil says as he sets our lunch down on his desk. "You should go take your lunch."

Camila shoots daggers at me, but I don't react. I refuse to let her get to me.

"If you're sure you won't need me."

She pushes off the desk and bats her eyes at my husband—right in front of me.

"I think we can handle any wrong numbers on our own," I say before turning my back on her to start unpacking our food.

Camila doesn't say another word. The only sound heard is the door slam on her way out.

"What's all this for?" Gil asks as he sits in his chair.

"I was in the neighborhood, so I thought I'd come to surprise my husband at work."

"In the neighborhood?" He raises his eyebrows.

I round his desk and lean over him, placing my hands on the armrests of his leather chair. The way I'm positioned gives him an unrestricted view of the black lace bra I'm wearing. He's taking full advantage of the scenery as I lean in to kiss him.

"Lizzie," he says between kisses. "We're in my office."

"I'm quite aware of where we are."

"We can't do this here."

"Why not?" I stand up and sway my hips as I walk across his office. "I'll lock the door."

"The walls are thin."

"I'll be quiet." I flash a smile over my shoulder.

"I don't know," Gil says nervously.

I lock the door before turning back to my husband. As I walk back toward him, I unbutton my shirt and allow it to fall to the ground. Gil's frozen in place; his eyes glued to my body. Now, I have his full attention, and I plan on taking advantage of it.

Mr. Benton is about to see how good spontaneity can be.

9

Gilbert

When Lizzie leaves the office, I realize we didn't even touch the food she ordered. I straighten my shirt quickly before I rush out to catch her.

"Liz," I call right as she's about to step into the elevator.

"Yes?" She turns around.

"Here's your sandwich. I don't want it to go to waste."

"Thank you." She takes the sandwich and looks over my shoulder. "Sorry, we didn't get to eat."

"I'm not sorry in the least," I say quietly. "I love you, Lizzie."

"Love you more," she says and gives me one last kiss before she gets into the waiting elevator.

When I turn around to head back into my office, Liam sits at his desk, grinning from ear to ear.

"You might need to wipe your face, Mr. Benton," Liam says and points to my cheek. "You have a little something red there."

I'm sure Lizzie left some lipstick behind, but I don't care. I feel like I'm on top of the world right now.

Camila, however, is standing in the hall, arms crossed. I feel like I'm stuck in the middle of some weird competition between these two.

She also managed to catch me off guard—but this time, I liked it.

10

Elizabeth

L unch, at least that's what we'll call it, was a huge success. I'm on cloud nine when I get home. I rush straight to the office to update my blog. But first, I read through the replies on my last post asking for suggestions.

There are so many replies it takes me over an hour to get through them. They range from charming ideas such as ice skating or a romantic dinner to very spicy ideas that involve blindfolds and handcuffs. My readers have vivid imaginations.

Operation Stake My Claim was a success! Gil had no idea his afternoon appointment was a lunch date with his wife. A girl doesn't kiss and tell, but I will say we didn't get much eating done—I brought my lunch home with me. And I'm quite certain the woman who thought my husband was up for grabs got my message to stay away loud and clear. The best part of all—Gil and I had fun.

My next question is, how do I keep the momentum going? ~Lizzie

I hit send and then switch to my personal social media page and scroll down my wall. While I'm commenting on a few of my friends' posts, I get a notification that I have a reply already.

Dear Lizzie, Way to go, girl. I love hearing your stories. If only we all were as brave as you. I think you should start a website where you give dating ideas. You know, to help out other couples who need to spice things up. Keeping the romance alive is a hard job. ~M.

A website that gives date ideas to couples. Hmm. That's an interesting idea, but I wouldn't even know where to start. Then it hits me. Maybe this is something Gil and I could do together? It would fulfill his need for planning and structure while filling my need for thinking out of the box. It could be just what we need to rekindle the flame between us.

I spend the rest of the afternoon writing up a business proposition Gil won't be able to say no to—or at least I hope he won't say no to. He's not much of a social media kind of guy. Because of his job, he's forced to use social media, but for his personal life, he'd rather stay out of the spotlight. I'm hoping that if he's in charge of the planning and I'm responsible for the actual website, we'll both have fun and reconnect at the same time.

My phone dings with a text.

(Gil) Don't cook. I'm bringing dinner home.

(Lizzie) Sounds perfect.

Gil's car pulls up right around seven p.m. I haven't been able to sit still all day. I'm bursting with excitement.

"Honey, I'm home," Gil calls as he walks in the front door.

"I missed you." I reach out and hug him. "What did you bring home? It smells delicious."

"Italian food, from that little restaurant you like so much."

My stomach decides to growl. "Yum. I'm starving."

I set the table while Gil unpacks the bag. He even bought a bottle of red wine to go with dinner.

"I thought maybe after dinner you could put on the little black number that I didn't get to see the other night," Gil says, a hopeful smile on his face.

"I think that can be arranged."

While we eat dinner, Gil tells me about the rest of his afternoon. It was full of phone calls and paperwork.

"What did you do after you got home?"

"Well." I take a sip of my wine. "I did some blogging, and I came up with an idea I want to run by you."

Gil leans forward. "You've piqued my interested."

I tell Gil how I want to start a website aimed at people who are already a couple but may be struggling to keep the romance alive.

"You know how hard it is to squeeze in adult time, especially when there's little kids around or if a couple just never put a focus on it, to begin with," I say. "I'd like to offer people a place where they can go to find practical yet fun and creative activities for couples. Out of the box kind of ideas."

Gil takes a bite of food and chews slowly. He appears to be mulling over everything I just said. "And how will we know if these date ideas are any good?"

We'll try them out on ourselves." I smile.

So, we're going to be the guinea pigs for your website idea?"

I"guess that's one way to put it. I'd prefer to look at it as investing in our relationship."

11

Gilbert

Lizzie's sitting across from me trying to convince me to start some sort of a dating website, where we'll be case study number one. I don't know whether she's crazy or brilliant.

I listen carefully while she tells me the plan.

We'll come up with creative, out-of-the-box, date ideas," she says. "The dates will require both people to take an active role."

So, no dinner and a movie?"

"Dinner and a movie is a great date, but we'll put our own twist on it." She stops and appears to be thinking. "Dinner wouldn't be just ordering out but maybe trying a new recipe together or packing a floor picnic. The movie doesn't have to be in a theater. It could be a backyard 'drive-in' if the couple has a projector or popcorn and cuddling at home with a movie the couple has either never watched or that they know every word to—in that case, if they end up not watching it." She waggles her eyebrows. "They won't be missing anything."

I sit back and watch my wife. Her smile lights up her face. Her blue eyes are dancing with excitement. This is something she really wants to do.

She's already proven with her blog that she's not only good at being online, but she's also comfortable with it. Me, not so much. Who am I kidding? Not at all. I'm forced to be online professionally for my day job, but that's where it ends. I don't have any personal social media accounts at all. This idea of hers is so far out of my comfort zone.

However, we promised each other when the kids moved out; we'd focus on each other. Up to this point, I've done a poor job of upholding my end of the agreement. I've spent the past six months moping around, not even trying. It's taken a toll on our relationship. Lizzie's been feeling neglected and hurt. That's the last thing I ever want her to feel.

Before I know it's happening, the words are coming out of my mouth. "Sure. I think it'll be fun."

"Oh, Gil." She jumps out of her chair and throws her arms around my neck. "Thank you so much. You won't regret it."

"I know something else I won't regret."

"And what's that?"

"Seeing you in that sexy black lingerie that I can't wait to peel you out of."

12

Gilbert

L iz is fast asleep in my arms. And I'm wide awake with my thoughts. What was I thinking? I just agreed to participate in putting our private life on the internet. The smile on Lizzie's face told me how much she wants this, but I'm not cut out for being in the spotlight. It's bad enough to have my picture and a bio up on the city's website. I wish I could take it back. But I know that's not possible. She has her heart set on doing this.

When I finally fall asleep, my dreams transport me to some crazy, mixed-up place somewhere between reality and virtual reality. Our cell phones and computers come alive and watch our every move. Cameras pop out of the walls. People have their faces pressed against the glass as they watch us through our windows as if we're a circus sideshow. Each time I startle awake in a cold sweat until I decide sleep isn't worth it, and I climb out of bed.

It's six a.m., an early wake-up, but I don't mind. I pull the French press out of the cupboard and start some coffee. I haven't made my usual Saturday breakfast in months. That's going to change today. Gathering the ingredients, I prepare to make French toast with caramelized bananas, bacon, and fresh fruit. Then, I start cooking. Doing something so familiar feels good and calms that part of me that was so unsettled all night.

"You're up early." Liz comes up behind me, startling me.

"I couldn't sleep." I kiss her good morning. "So, I thought I'd make us a nice breakfast."

"I've missed our Saturday breakfasts." Lizzie pours us each a cup of coffee, adding just the right amounts of sugar and creamer. "I dreamt about our new website all night. It's going to be amazing."

"I dreamt about it too."

"You don't seem too happy." She takes her mug of steaming coffee and sits at the kitchen table.

"Liz, I know I said yes," I say as I put the food onto paper plates. "But the more I think about it, the more I don't feel like it's a good idea."

"Oh," she says and looks down at her plate. "What don't you like about it?""I don't want to be front and center, sharing our personal lives with everyone."

"It won't be like that. We'll be thinking up the date ideas and trying them out to see how they work, but nothing about us will be on the site." She takes a bite of French toast. "Oh my gosh, this is delicious." Liz is momentarily distracted. "It won't be a personal thing, like the blog. This new site will be a business venture."

"And what do you plan to call this, business venture?" I tilt my head waiting to hear her answer.

"I like the name Real Life Romance. Because it will be real-life couples, like you and me, trying to keep the romance alive—in real life." She giggles.

Real Life Romance. I'll admit, it's a catchy name. Maybe it won't be that bad as long as we aren't documenting personal stuff. "Okay, we can give it a try."

"Perfect." She claps her hands. "I've already purchased the domain name and did a rough draft of an introduction. I didn't hit publish, so it's not live."

"I guess you were pretty certain I'd say yes." I can't help but smile. Liz's tenacity and zest for life are something I've always admired.

"I was hoping you would." She shrugs. "And now you did, so everything's good."

We work together to get the breakfast dishes washed and the kitchen back in order. After we get dressed, I follow her into her office so she can show me what she's come up with.

She sits in the comfy gaming chair I bought her for her birthday last year and opens her laptop.

"I did a search for dating websites for married couples, and all that came up were sites advertising discrete affairs." She wrinkles her nose. "Obviously, that's not what we're after here."

"Definitely not," I agree.

Liz's fingers fly across the keyboard as she types. Then she slides the laptop so that I can see the screen.

When Liz said she wrote an introduction, that's all I was expecting to see. However, realliferomance.org looks more like a professionally designed website. The landing page, where her introduction message is placed, is bright and welcoming.

Congratulations! You've finally reached the momentous point in your relationship. The one you've both dreaded and looked forward to for so long—the kids have moved out! You are officially empty nesters.

For years, your imagination has run wild with all the exciting things you and your partner can do now that you're alone, but instead of living your dreams, you realize you're stuck. Stuck in old patterns, old habits, old routines.

You've tried everything you could think of with no success, and now you've taken your quest to the internet—and found us! Real Life Romance offers you creative ideas and activities designed to reopen the lines of communication that are intended to stoke the fire to rekindle your romance.

The next question you're asking is how much will this cost? At Real Life Romance, we believe budget shouldn't stand in the way of taking your relationship to the next level. We offer several different options, from no-cost services to premium services. You choose the one that fits you best. And there's no monthly membership or hidden fees.

What do I do next?

You've already taken the first step by finding us. Our suggestion is to start with the ice breaker, Getting to Know You (Again). It's a fun, low-key activity designed to kick-start communication. There are two ways to play. 1. Use the list online, or you can print it. It's that simple.

Now, it's time to play.

Grab some dinner and wine, if you like. Read the questions aloud and take turns answering. You'll quickly learn these aren't your garden variety of getting-to-know-you questions. We've worked hard to develop creative and fun questions to help you learn new things about each other.

There's a lot of questions, so don't feel pressure to answer them all in one sitting. You can do as few or as many as you want, and you can come back to them at any time. Getting to Know You

(Again) is meant to be fun and to spark conversation—the first step in reconnecting. So, take your time and have fun.

When you're ready, the other tabs have ideas for date night activities, and we'll soon have pre-made date boxes you can purchase.

Below the introduction are the links that bring you to the questions. One is to print the list. The other takes you to another page on the site where the questions are listed.

There are two other tabs: Do-it-Yourself Dates and Pre-made Date Boxes. Both pages say coming soon.

"You've really thought this through." As usual, I'm impressed with my wife's ingenuity. She's always possessed an innate ability to think outside the box.

"It's not much, just a beginning idea." She shrugs. "What do you think?"

"I think it's brilliant."

13

Elizabeth

"Do you want to try it out?" I ask, hopeful Gil's up to having some fun.

"Sure." He doesn't hesitate to respond.

"Do you want to do them online or print them?"

I don't know why I ask. I already know what his choice will be.

"Ideally I'd prefer to print them," Gil answers. "But for right now, let's do them online."

The second part of his answer surprises me, but I happily go with it.

Grabbing the laptop, we go downstairs. We've just eaten, and it's a bit early for wine, so we settle for bottles of water. Then, we get comfy on the couch and start the questions.

"The first one is easy," I say. "What's your favorite season?"

"Summer," Gil answers.

"Mine too."

We both love to spend as much time as possible outdoors. Living in the city, we don't have a big yard, but we manage to use every inch to plant a vegetable garden and flowers.

"My turn." Gil scrolls down some and picks a question. "Here's a good one. What's the first thing you found attractive about me?"

I smile and am transported back to when I was sixteen years old. It was the middle of a school day, right after lunch. Kelly and I had lockers next to each other. We were grabbing the books for our afternoon classes when Gil and Chris rounded the corner. It was my junior year, and I don't know how I never saw him before. But it was just like in the movies when everything else blurs, and it was only Gil and me. The first thing I noticed was his long reddish-brown hair—I've always been a sucker for a ginger. I leaned over to Kelly and whispered that I was going to marry that boy. She looked and me and started laughing. Not a quiet laugh, a full fit of head-turning laughter. That's what got their attention and is how Gil and I met for the first time.

"My hair?" he asks, surprised.

"Yes, your hair." I reach out and run my fingers through it. "I still love your hair. What about you?"

"I don't know if you want the real answer or the appropriate answer?""Both."

"I was a sixteen-year-old guy." He blushes. "You had a low-cut T-shirt shirt on. I couldn't take my eyes off your breasts."

His comment makes me laugh, especially because I remember it so well. Kelly was still cackling when the boys stopped in front of us. Chris got his dander up. He wanted to know why Kelly was laughing at them. By this point, she had tears running down her face—I don't know why she found my comment that funny.

Meanwhile, Gil and I just stared at each other. Well, I was looking at his face because after his hair, I noticed his incredible, amber-colored eyes. Gil's gaze, on the other hand, took quite a while to make its way up to my face.

"Next question. If you could pick one superpower, what would it be?"

"Mind control," he answers, deadpan. "This way, I could make everyone do what I want, and life would be organized and scheduled."

"Only you, Gil." I chuckle."What?" He shrugs.

"When given a chance to fly, have super strength, or any number of amazing powers, you go with schedules and organization." I smile.

Over the next few hours, we take turns asking all sorts of questions. We share a lot of laughs and recall some fun memories.

"What did you think about it?" I ask, hoping to get Gil's input.

"I thought it was a lot of fun," he answers. "They're not the typical, 'what's your favorite color' questions. I like that."

"I know we only got through the first bunch," I say. "But if you look further through them, they range from innocent to steamy."

"One issue I see is the questions aren't mixed too well. It's almost like they're grouped by categories. I think it would work better if the questions were more random."

Gil has a good point.

"How do we fix it?"It doesn't take long for us to figure out an easy solution for the printed questions. Gil opens the original file and adds dotted lines between the questions.

"We can go back and update the directions," I suggest. "I like the idea of cutting them apart and putting them in a jar. The couple can plan a time to do the activity, or if they're more spontaneous, they can grab one any time."

"That's a great idea. I'll call Brian for the website," Gil suggests.

Brian is Kelly's husband. He works in IT and builds websites in his spare time.

"I'm sure there's a plug-in that can generate the questions randomly on the website."

This is exactly what makes Gil and me such a good team. We complement each other's strengths and weaknesses. As long we're together, there's nothing we can't accomplish.

14

Gilbert

Liz compiled a great variety of questions. With some tweaking, making the category of the question random, we can take this ice-breaker to the next level. Look at me, Mr. Organization, wanting to do something random.

"What are the do-it-yourself dates all about?" I ask. This one has me intrigued.

"My section is for the more hands-on couple. Rather than buying a pre-made date box, this section will have downloadable files," Liz explains.

I don't know how Liz comes up with these ideas. She tells me this section will present themed dates from simple to extravagant with instructions on carrying out the date and what supplies are needed. It will be up to the couples to put everything together and allows them a lot of room to customize their experience.

"I'd like to have a mix where some dates require both partners to play an equal role in the planning. Others will require only one person to plan as a surprise for their partner."

I watch my wife in complete awe as she animatedly tells me all her ideas. I don't know how she's come up with so much in such a short time.

She goes on to explain her thoughts on the pre-packaged dates. These are going to need a lot more work. Not only do we need the date theme, but we also need the inventory to make up the actual boxes.

"I think it'd be wise if we take this part slowly until we know we're getting website traffic, I suggest. "We can try one or two and see how they do before we go crazy there."

"That works for me."

Liz and I are communicating and working together for the first time in months. This is the way we always were, the way we're supposed to be, and it feels good.

We spend the rest of the afternoon coming up with date themes, breaking them down step-by-step, and adding a twist. Before I know it, it's dark outside and well past dinnertime.

"I think I owe you dinner and wine," I suggest.

Liz's eyes open wide. "Like as in we're going out on a date?"

"Just like that, yes."

"Give me ten minutes to freshen up."

Liz springs up from the couch and runs up the steps. She complains that she's getting old, but she still moves like she's in her twenties. I'm sure she wants to hurry, so I don't have a chance to change my mind. While I don't like knowing that, I understand. I've just suggested we do something last minute, an uncharacteristic move on my part. However, it still feels like it's in my comfort zone. In my head, it's dinner time, and we need to eat, so that's exactly what we're going to do.

15

Elizabeth

I don't want to give Gil a chance to back out, so I rush upstairs to change my shirt and fix my hair. It doesn't take more than five minutes before I'm back downstairs.

Thankfully, we bundled up because it's pretty chilly out. Flurries blow in the cold breeze. Living in a bigger city has its perks, one of which is having so many restaurant options within walking distance.

Three blocks from our house is a little restaurant called Essence. The chef/owners focus on presenting quality meals while practicing sustainability. Because of this, their menu is constantly changing. We've been coming here for years and have never been disappointed.

Tonight, we both order poached salmon and a winter salad with a caramelized honey dressing. Gil orders a bottle of his favorite oak-aged chardonnay that pairs perfectly with the salmon. We enjoy the relaxed atmosphere as we eat our dinner. Our conversation drifts back to Real Life Romance, and we decide to add a "Last Minute Dinner-Date" to the Do-it-Yourself list.

Gil's on a role with ideas, so I take notes on my phone because I know I'll never remember everything he's saying. For someone who doesn't like spur-of-the-moment-things, he seems to be enjoying himself. He reminds me several times that meals aren't spontaneous things. We eat dinner every evening. It may be a technicality, but I'll let him have this one.

After our meal, we walk, hand in hand, back to our house. This is exactly how I pictured our life after the kids moved out.

It feels like a dream.

And the dream only gets better once we get inside. Gil helps me take off my coat, but he doesn't stop there. He helps me right out of my clothes and makes love to me on the sofa.

Afterward, Gil pulls the ivory sherpa blanket over us, and we fall asleep in a mix of tangled limbs.

16

Gilbert

I'm in that fuzzy area that's between sleep and awake. The place where you can hear things, but aren't sure if it's from your dreams or reality.

"Oh, God. My eyes," Hunter exclaims.

I jump awake and see the blanket has slid down. Liz's breasts are uncovered. And our twenty-four-year-old son is standing in our living room with his hands over his eyes. Quickly, I pull the blanket up, covering Liz. She grabs my hand, pulling me to her.

"Liz, wake up." I shake her shoulder.

"I don't want to," she says, eyes still closed.

"Hunter's here."

"I need brain bleach," Hunter yells as he turns his back on us.Liz shoots up, holding the blanket close to her body.

"Hunter, what are you doing here?" she asks, panicked. "We didn't know you were coming over today."

"That's obvious. I'm never going to be able to sit on that couch again."

I scramble to find my clothes which are in a pile mixed with Liz's. I'm hopping on one foot, trying to get dressed quickly while tossing Liz her clothes. She starts laughing hysterically.

Why is she laughing? There's nothing funny about this situation. This is exactly what happens when we do something out of the ordinary. What was I thinking?

In between her fits of laughter, she slides her clothes back on.

"We're decent now. You can turn back around."

"What were you two thinking?" Hunter scolds us.

"Your father and I were—"

"No, mom. Stop. I already get what you guys were up to. I don't need the specifics."

Liz shakes her head. "I wasn't going to give details, but why are you acting so shocked. None of you would exist if we didn't do that."

My head bounces back and forth following their banter.

"Come on, sit down." I motion for Hunter to join me on the couch.

"How about we sit at the table?" Hunter avoids the couch like the plague and heads straight for the kitchen.

"Are you two hungry? I can make something for brunch," I offer and start grabbing ingredients for homemade waffles.

"That sounds great. I'll be there in a minute," Liz says as she finishes folding the blanket.

When she comes into the kitchen, she kisses Hunter's cheek as she passes him on the way to put the coffee on. "To what do we owe this unexpected visit?"

"I have some good news I wanted to tell you guys."

"Oh. What's up?" I ask.

"Well." He hesitates. "I've been applying for new jobs."

"You have?" I'm surprised by his revelation. I thought he liked his job.

"How do I say this?" Hunter mumbles.

Liz sits at the table across from him. "Is something wrong?"

Hunter fidgets with his hands; his eyes dart around like he did when he was little and he didn't want to tell us something.

Leaving the bowl with the waffle batter on the counter, I join my wife and son at the table. Then, Hunter proceeds to shock me.

"I met a girl on a dating app," he says quickly. "We've been seeing each other for the past year."

A year ago? He met a girl last year, and he hasn't said anything to us about it.

"She lives in Florida," he continues. "We've been flying back and forth to see each other."

Well, now his impromptu trip to Cocoa Beach over the holidays makes more sense.

The more he talks, the more aggravated I get. How could he keep something like this from us? And for an entire year? I look over to Liz, hoping to find support, but instead, she's smiling.

I've held my tongue as long as I could.

"And you didn't think to tell us?" I ask.

"At first, we just talked a lot. We didn't want to rush anything with how far apart we live."

"That's understandable," Liz says.

"But then we started to visit each other. The more time we spent together, the more we've grown to care about each other."

"Tell us about her," Liz encourages.

"Well, her name is Emerie."

Hunter tells us she's twenty-three and is a kindergarten teacher. Her family lives in Florida, and she's an only child. He pulls out his phone and hands it to Liz. I lean over and see a picture of Hunter and a petite blonde.

"She's gorgeous," Liz says and passes the phone back to him.

"She is." Hunter beams.

"But what does this have to do with a new job?"

Maybe I should, but I don't expect to hear the next part of what Hunter tells us.

"I found an IT job. The company is headquartered in Florida. I'll be working remotely for the next month or so." He looks between us. "Then, I'll be moving."

Liz gets up and wraps her arms around her son. "I'm so happy for you. When can we meet her?"

"She's flying up when school goes on Spring break. Then, we're going to drive back together."

First, Grace decides to go to Hawaii for school. Now, Hunter's moving to Florida. Why couldn't he do things like I did? Find a job and a girl close to home.

"Dad. You haven't said anything."

"I'm taking it all in."

That's putting it mildly. My brain is a scrambled mess. Just last night, I thought I was finally on the right track. I even did something spontaneous, only to have it ruined this morning. Now, my son is telling me he's moving to Florida for a girl.

Liz grabs my hand. "Dad and I are very happy for you, and we can't wait to meet her. Right, Gil?" She squeezes, encouraging me to give a polite response.

"Yes. Very happy." I stand and return to the bowl on the counter. "I'm going to finish cooking."

"Is he okay?" Gil whispers to his mom.

"You know your dad. It might take him a little bit, but he'll be just fine."

17

Elizabeth

Brian was able to write code or do a plug-in. I'm not sure what computer-ish magic he did, but now the Re-Getting to Know You questions are on a random generator. I'm amazed by it and keep clicking the button.

All week I've worked on taking our notes for the Do-it-Yourself-Dates and inputting them onto the website. Each is set up so when the couple purchases the date they'll get a digital download with the instructions. Although the site is still basic, I hit publish, and within seconds it's out there for the whole digital universe to see.

Then, I head to my blog to give an update.

Hello Tribespeople. I know I missed a week, and I apologize for that. Life has thrown a few curve balls our way the past two weeks. Our second oldest son surprised us with a visit. He told us that he not only got a new job, but he also met a girl. A year ago. And that he's moving to Florida to be with her. Wow—right? It was a huge surprise, but if you saw the way his face lit up when he talked about her, you'd be as happy as I am for him.

On the marriage front, one of my readers gave me the idea of starting a website for couples who want to rekindle their romance or just want some creative date ideas. So, I did it. I'd like to introduce you all to RealLifeRomance.org.

I can tell you from experience the Re-Getting to Know You questions are a lot of fun. I highly recommend trying them. The Last-Minute Dinner Date was actually Gil's idea—yes, I know the words 'last-minute' and 'Gil's idea' in the same sentence are quite unusual. I was shocked. It's a really great idea for people who tend to get nervous with last minute plans. As Gil explained, dinner is something we do every day, so it isn't really spontaneous. We tried this out last night and had a great time—during dinner and after.

Some other features will be coming soon, including the opportunity to purchase a ready-made date box. If you get a few minutes, check out the site and let me know your thoughts. What things would you like to see?Hit me with your ideas.

~Lizzie

Gil's in the basement in his workshop. I think he's still trying to deal with Hunter's big news. Working with his hands to build things has always been his go-to when he needs to calm down and re-center himself. He's made several pieces of our furniture, including our four-poster bed. When Marco and Ivy got engaged two years ago, he started working on a cedar chest to give them for their wedding. Unfortunately, his day job keeps him so busy he doesn't get much time to go down there. Hopefully, a few hours of quiet doing what he loves will benefit him.

While Gil is busy, I occupy myself with the website. I have some ideas that I think will be fun Do-It-Yourself-Dates. I'm trying to think of some out-of-the-box dates or at least some unique twists for more specific dates. So far, I've come up with Pretend to be a Tourist in Your Hometown—something that can work in both a big and small town. Video Game Night, because adults like to chill and have fun. Spice It Up, taking a couples' intimacy class. There are several places in Philly, and I've found some online aimed at instructing and educating couples on various sex-positive subjects. The last one is Karaoke Night, either at home or on the town—this one also can be a double date.

With a double date in mind, I text Kelly.

(Liz) Do you and Brian have plans Friday?

(Kelly) I don't think so. Why?

(Liz) Want to go to Music Café for karaoke?

(Kelly) Haha. Gil is going to go to karaoke?.

Singing in front of people isn't exactly one of Gil's go-to activities, but we're trying new things, right?

(Liz) Yep, he'll go.

(Kelly) We wouldn't miss it!

Perfect. I'll call you later in the week, and we'll figure out the details.

I hope I can get Gil on board. I haven't done karaoke since I was in high school. This is going to be so much fun.

18

Gilbert

It's taken all week to put myself back together from Hunter's surprise visit last Sunday. Just when I thought everything was back to the status quo, Lizzie wants to try another date—karaoke. I've never done karaoke in my life, and I'm content to keep it that way. But I promised Liz I'd go along with these crazy date ideas, and admittedly, some of them have been fun. So, now I find myself walking out the door with my wife to meet Kelly and Brian at Music Café for snacks and singing.

The place is packed with dozens of people our kids' ages.

"Why don't we go someplace else?" I lean in close so Liz can hear me above the music.

"Why?"

I look around the room. "We're the oldest people in here.""So what?" She leans in and kisses me.

So what? We could be these kids' parents. I pull out my phone and open a webpage to do a search. There has to be somewhere else people our age hang out.

"Gil, loosen up." Kelly elbows me. "Want to sing with me?"

"No." My immediate decline of her offer makes her laugh.

Without missing a beat, Kelly grabs Brian's hand and drags the poor guy to the stage. There's one person ahead of them. While they wait, Kelly looks through the song list and points out a song. Brian nods in agreement. When it's their turn, they take the stage, and their performance begins.

Neither of them would be chosen for American Idol, but I don't think they care. They're in their own world as they belt out Sonny and Cher's, I Got You, Babe. I watch, entranced by the way Brian gazes at his wife and she at him. They don't care about their vocal abilities or that they're in a room full of college-aged kids. They are engrossed in the moment and with each other.

Liz and I used to have that—an ease with one another. Lately, things feel different between us. I can't put my finger on it, but something feels off. I'm envious of Brian and Kelly.

"Will you sing with me?" Liz asks.

My heart pounds so hard, I'm afraid it's going to break free of my chest. I knew she was going to want me to sing with her. All day I've been trying to talk myself into it. Liam noticed my nerves and offered the advice my parents gave me back in middle school when I had to give an oral report—imagine everyone in their underwear. But right now, none of that matters. I'm glued to my seat. There's no way I can do it.

"I'm gonna pass."

"Whatever." Liz rolls her eyes and struts over to the side of the stage where there's now a small group gathering.

A few of the young guy's heads turn as my wife walks by. I know Liz lacks confidence in her looks, but clearly, I'm not the only man who thinks she's a knockout.

Liz is always concerned about her extra curves, the fine lines on her face, and the extra hairs that grow on her lip. It seems like she's in a constant battle against her body. I'll do anything and everything to support her so she can feel confident about herself even though I don't see any of what she considers 'problems.' When I look at her, all I see is a confident, beautiful woman. I only wish she would see herself the way I see her.

Kelly and Brian return to the table.

"Earth to Gilbert," Kelly says as she sits down.

"Aren't you going to sing with Liz?" Brian asks.

"Me? No. I can't sing."

"And I can?" Brian laughs. "It's not about being able to sing. It's doing something special with your wife."

Liz steps onto the stage and the music comes on.

"If you don't, someone else will."

Brian motions to the stage where Liz is now joined by some good-looking young guy who watches her intently as he sings the opening lyrics to Lady Gaga's Shallow. Then it's Liz's turn. She opens her mouth, and pitch-perfect lyrics come out.

Liz took chorus in high school and always got the solos. Everyone encouraged her to pursue a career in the music industry, but Liz would hear nothing of it. Seeing her shine on stage right now makes me wonder why she didn't choose that path. Did my desire to marry young and start a family right away influence her decision?

The music ends, and the café erupts in applause. I realize I missed most of her performance because I was lost in my head.

The kid on the stage with Liz offers his hand to help her down the few steps leading back to the café floor. He walks her back toward the table and then touches her arm.

"Could I interest you in grabbing a drink with me?"

I jump up from my seat. "She's married." In a possessive move, I put my arm around her waist and pull her close to me.

He holds his hands up. "I'm sorry. I didn't realize."

Liz smiles kindly. "It's okay. Thanks for the song."

"Yep." He walks away with his proverbial tail between his legs.

Liz nuzzles into my side. "Are you jealous, Gilbert Benton?

"Very."

"You're the only man I've ever wanted."

I puff my chest out with pride. I want to climb onto the table and announce to everyone in the room that this amazing woman is here with me. But my bravado quickly dies and is replaced by the more timid, nervous man I naturally am. Instead, I pull out her seat, allowing her to sit. Then, I slide my seat a little closer to her and put my arm around her. If I can't bring myself to get on stage or loudly announce my claim, the least I can do is quietly show her my affection.

Throughout the evening, we enjoy tapas and conversation with our friends while people take turns at the microphone.

It's after one a.m. when we finally get home. Lizzie kicks off her heels as soon as she's inside the house.

I grab my cellphone from my pocket and pull up my playlist. End of the Road by Boyz II Men starts to play.

"May I have this dance?" I ask and offer her my hand.

"I'd love to." She places her tiny hand in mine.

Pulling my wife close to me, we sway to the music while I sing quietly for only Liz to hear.

19

Elizabeth

S o, you see, fellow tribemates, Gil may not do things in the way
I'd expect. Take, for instance, this weekend. We double-dated
with some good friends. Our destination—is a karaoke café. My
friend and her husband couldn't wait and took the stage together
the minute we arrived, and although her husband's vocals are,
well, let's just say he's not going to be offered a recording contract
any time soon, but it didn't matter. They didn't care what anyone
else in the room thought. They sang their hearts out to one
another. I have to admit. I was feeling jealous.

I asked Gil to sing with me, but just as I thought, he said
'no.' It felt like the one step forward two steps back kinda thing.
Although I was upset, I didn't let it stop me. I haven't sung on a
stage in ages, and I wasn't going to pass up this opportunity. Part
of me secretly hoped Gil would get past his fear and join me, but
things didn't work out that way. Instead, I sang a duet with some
twenty-something college boy who asked me to get a drink with
him after we sang.

I won't lie. It was flattering. The best part was Gil's reaction.

Just like in all the romance novels, Gil stood up and got all
possessive, pulling me close to him and chased the guy away.
He made my heart pitter-patter. My stomach get butterflies.
Suddenly, it didn't matter that he didn't sing with me. In that one
move, he made me feel like the most special woman in the room.

And if you think that was good, the best was yet to come.

We stayed out until after midnight. Don't laugh. We're old. My feet were sore from the heels I wore. All I wanted to do was get home, kick them off, change into some warm, comfy pj's, and crawl into bed. But then End of the Road, our wedding song, began playing through Gil's phone. Right there in our living room, we danced together. While he held me tight, he sang softly in my ear, just like he did the day he married me.

Here, I was feeling sorry for myself. I thought our karaoke date was a failure, but I was wrong. Gil didn't participate in karaoke the way I thought. No, he did it in a manner totally unique to him—to us.

Karaoke date was a huge win!

Lesson for the day- don't put your partner in a well-constructed box of how you think they should act or what you think they should do. Allow them the freedom to be who they are. That might be the best thing you can do for your relationship. ~Lizzie

We've only just scratched the surface of starting this website and experimenting with different date ideas, but I can already feel a bit of a shift. We're growing closer, just like I'd hoped.

"Liz, are you here?" Gil calls.

Closing my laptop, I call, "I'm here." I make my way downstairs quickly. "What are you doing home?"

"I forgot my lunch and decided we'd just come here to eat."

"We?" I look around.

"Don't freak out. I'm on the road with Camila today."

"I see." Fire rages inside me at the mention of her name. "Where is she?"

"She's finishing up a call. She'll be in shortly."

"Wonderful." I open the fridge. "What can I make you?"

"A sandwich will be fine." Gil grabs a soda and sits at the kitchen table.

The front door opens, and I hear the clicking of heels on the hardwood floor.

"Knock. Knock. I hope it was okay I let myself in?" She gives my appearance a judgmental perusal.

I wasn't expecting company, and since the only things on my agenda were a blog entry and housecleaning, I'm wearing Gil's old sweatpants and a T-shirt, my hair pulled back in a messy ponytail. On the other hand, Camila is wearing heels, a black pencil skirt, and a button-down version of her uniform shirt. Although I'm curious how she conducts inspections in an outfit like that, I don't ask. The less I hear her voice, the better.

Right now, though, I wish Gil had given me a heads-up. I would've changed and made myself look more presentable. Instead, I'm at a disadvantage and am left feeling self-conscious.

Like a shark, Camila smells blood in the water and goes on the offensive.

"Did Gil not let you know we were on our way?" she asks, a fake sincerity lacing her tone. "Gil, you should've let her know so she had the chance to change out of her pajamas." Camila comes over to the counter where I'm making Gil's lunch. "I can finish that if you'd like to go get dressed."

It may only be a butterknife, but I set it down on the counter, so I'm not tempted to stab her with it.

"That's so sweet of you, but I am dressed."

"Oh, dear." She puts her hand over her heart, feigning shock. "I'm so sorry."

"Would you like a sandwich?" I grudgingly ask.

"I brought a salad." She holds up a small lunch bag. "I'd have to spend twice the amount of time at the gym if I ate sandwiches." Then, she turns and takes a seat across from Gil.

Why did he bring her here? Being a woman is hard enough without having people like her thrown in my face. We're constantly barraged with messages of how we should be skinnier, have the right hair color and cut, eat a certain way, and have a career, among many other unspoken rules. Some days it feels like no matter what choice we make, it's never right.

Those I choose to allow into my small circle of friends believe that life is hard enough. Instead of cutting each other down, we build each other up because we realize we're stronger together. Women like Camila don't subscribe to that theory. She's content to stomp on anyone to get what she wants.

I finish Gil's sandwich and bring it to him.

"Thank you, babe." Gil grabs my arm and kisses my cheek.

"Oh, look how sweet you two are." Camila's voice is like nails on a chalkboard.

"Are you going to eat?" he asks.

"I finished my lunch right before you got here," I lie. There's no way I can swallow food in her presence.

"You'll at least sit with us, right?"

"Of course."

The lunch conversation is tense. Being polite to this woman is draining.

As soon as Gil finishes, I get up and clear his place, thankful for being able to step away from the table for even a moment.

Gil looks at his watch. "We need to get going, or we're going to be late for our appointment."

"I'm glad you stopped by."

"Me too."

We walk to the front door, and Gil opens it to leave.

"Oh, I forgot my bag. I'll meet you at the car," Camila says and walks back into the kitchen.

"I'll see you after work." Gil kisses me and heads out to the car.

Camila comes back once Gil is outside, almost as though it were planned.

"If you think your little rendezvous at the office with Gil is going to deter me, you're sorely mistaken." She places her hand on her hip. "Gil's a smart man. Once he realizes he can have me, it won't take him long to see you're well past your expiration date. He'll leave you and never look back."

I'm shocked—my ability to form words is gone.

She opens the screen door.

"It was so nice to see you, Elizabeth. Thanks for your hospitality," she says loud enough, so Gil hears her sentiment.

He waves to me as they pull away.

Camila's words echo in my head. If it's her against me, I have nothing to fight with. She's young and beautiful, and she's right. I'm way past my expiration date.

Feeling defeated, I sit on the couch and cry.

20

Gilbert

I'm waiting for Camila outside the car. She had to go back and get her lunch bag. That woman is always forgetting something. On her way out, she stops and has an exchange with Liz. Although I can't hear what they're saying, from the look on Liz's face, the conversation doesn't appear positive.

Camila approaches, a big smile on her face. "Sorry about that." She opens the passenger door and slides in.

I look back to the house, but Liz has already closed the door.

"What did you say to Liz?"

"I thanked her for being so hospitable. After all, we were a disruption to her day."

Bringing Camila to the house might not have been the best idea. I know Liz isn't a fan. The only thing I was thinking about was surprising Liz and spending some extra time together.

Liz keeps saying she thinks Camila's after me; I don't see it, but if it's true, then Liz's visit to the office for lunch a few weeks ago should've put Camila in her place. I figured everything would be okay now, but based on the palpable tension during lunch, I think I was wrong.

I feel like I'm stuck between a rock and a hard place.

These days, I'm not usually on the road much, so I'm going to go with this situation isn't likely to happen again. I'll talk to Lizzie when I get home and hopefully smooth things over. And from here on out—keep these two women apart.

Camila and I arrive at the building to conduct today's inspection. A contractor is in the middle of renovating a block of houses. He found asbestos and had to have it remediated. Our job is to inspect the dwellings to ensure the air quality is at safe levels so his crew can get back to work. Camila hasn't done air testing yet, so I'm here to teach her how to conduct the tests properly. Then I'll observe her doing them on her own.

With a total of twenty units, this will take the rest of the afternoon. I did the first two units, and now Camila is completing them under my watch. The problem is, my mind keeps drifting back to my wife and the mess that was lunch.

We finish up right around four-thirty, which gives us just enough time to get back to the office and input our findings without having to stay too late.

I'm not a perfect man. I might make a lot of mistakes, but I try not to make the same mistake twice.

(Gil) We just got back to the office. It's going to take about forty-five minutes to upload all the info.

(Liz) Fine.

Oh no. One-word answers.

(Gil) We need to talk when I get home.

(Liz) About what?

(Gil) Camila

All day I've been repeating the scene in my head of Liz and Camila by the door.

Something was said that upset Liz.

(Liz) I'd rather not. I don't want to hear her name again.

(Gil) I'll be home as soon as I can.

I pull up at home and turn off the ignition. Before I get out of the car, I take a few breaths. I'm not sure what I'm walking into, but whatever it is, I'm pretty sure I deserve it. I screwed up bringing Camila to the house.

"Let's go, Gilbert. Can't put this off forever."

When I walk in, the aroma of homemade spaghetti sauce hits me. Liz is at the stove stirring the sauce. She has music playing and doesn't hear me come up behind her.

"Dinner smells incredible."

Liz jumps, nearly burning herself on the pot.

"You scared me to death." She giggles nervously.

"I'm sorry. I couldn't help it. I love coming home to my wife barefoot and in the kitchen." I grin.

She puts the pot of water on the induction burner.

"I didn't want to start the pasta until you got home."

Since Grace left, we've been sticking to quick and easy meals during the week. I wasn't expecting to see Liz making homemade sauce on a weekday. What's even more unusual is the homemade pasta hanging from the drying racks on the kitchen table.

"Is it a special occasion?"

"Does it need to be a special occasion for me to make pasta and sauce for my husband?"

"Well, no." I look at Liz, really look at her, and see the pain in her eyes. "What did Camila say to you before she left?"

"Nothing."

"Don't give me that, Liz." I take her hand. "I saw your face. I know she said something."

"She just reminded me of the differences between her and me." She pauses. "And that she's not through hitting on you."

"Lizzie, I'm sorry."

"Don't apologize for that b—"

"I'm apologizing for the mess that was lunch."

Liz doesn't respond. She turns away and goes to get the pasta.

"I'll do it." I carefully remove the long spaghetti from the rack and place it in the pot.

My brain is going a mile a minute while we eat dinner. Camila knew exactly how to strike my wife to make it hurt the most—her looks. It's something Liz struggles with daily. It still blows my mind, no matter how many times I try to understand it because I think my wife is beautiful. Unfortunately, all she sees is her flaws.

Then it comes to me, an idea for a pre-made date box. One that will stretch Liz, but that in the end, I think she'll enjoy—so will I.

"Gil, you still with me?" Liz asks.

"Sorry, I spaced out there."

"What were you thinking about?"

"A date box."

She puts her fork down. "You have my interest piqued."

"You're going to have to wait until it's together before you can see it."

Liz pouts.

"That's cute, but it's not going to get you anywhere this time."

"Fine. I'll wait." She sighs loudly.

After dinner, I go online to search for everything I'll need.

21

Elizabeth

Happy Friday, Tribe friends. This week has been something else. Tuesday, Gil brought the wicked witch home for lunch—they were on the road, and he didn't have food with him. Apparently, my visit with my husband at his office didn't discourage her as much as I thought it would. She made sure to point out all of my flaws and compared them to her youth. I hate saying it, and I'm gagging a little as I type this, but she is pretty and young. I can't compete with that. She's right. I'm trying to hold on to the fact that Gil loves me and not her.

Speaking of Gil and love. He informed me earlier this week that he's making our first pre-made date box. If all goes well, it will be the first one we offer on RealLifeRomance.org. All week he's been plotting and planning. And much to my dismay, he refuses to give me a single hint. Several unmarked packages have arrived in the mail. Before you ask, yes, I tried shaking them but got no clues as to the contents.

I'm expecting he'll give it to me tonight, because I'm told it's something we'll be doing this weekend. So......for all those who are now wondering with me—make sure you check back to see what the date is! ~Lizzie

Why does the clock move so slow? It must be the same principle as a watched pot never boils because every time I check the clock on my phone, time seems to be at a standstill. Just in case, I check to see if I missed any system updates. When I see none, I restart my phone in case the clock app isn't working correctly. Sadly, that doesn't help, and the seconds continue to tick by ever so slowly.

Finally, I hear Gil pull up at the house. My stomach fills with butterflies, and my heart rate picks up in anticipation. When I peek out the window, I see he's carrying a white box with a red ribbon tied around it. I feel like a child on Christmas morning. I'm ready to burst from anticipation

He's moving too slow, so I pull the door open, hoping to speed him up. It doesn't work. He continues his leisurely pace along the path. He's driving me crazy, and from the grin on his face, he knows it.

"Hurry up, please. I can't wait to open it."

He tilts his head just a bit. "This is for tomorrow, not tonight."

"What?" I whine.

Yep, just like a toddler.

But can you blame me? All week he's been building the suspense over this date box.

"You said I'd get to open it on the weekend. It's Friday and work is over, so it's the weekend," I complain some more, hoping he'll give in.

"Good try, sweetheart." Gil kisses my nose as he walks past me into the house. "There are still two more days to the weekend."

"You're a cruel man, Mr. Benton."

Gil belly laughs. "Trust me, Mrs. Benton. It will be worth the wait."

22

Elizabeth

After a very long night of waking up every hour and staring at the box that taunted me from the dresser, it's finally morning.

Gil has gotten back into our usual pattern of making a big cooked breakfast on Saturday mornings. I love his cooking and this tradition, but I would've been OK with instant oatmeal or toast—something quick. But no, he insists on a big breakfast and a relaxing pace.

After what feels like forever, we're finished eating, and the dishes are cleaned up.

Wait here," Gil instructs. "I'll be right back."

Yes, sir," I joke.

I"could get used to that," he calls over his shoulder and then laughs as he makes his way to our bedroom.

I hope he's getting the box because I don't know how much longer I can wait.

When he comes back into the kitchen, he is indeed carrying the date box which he sets on the table in front of me.

You'd think I'd rip right into it, but I find myself only staring at it, trying to imagine what's inside.

If you don't want to open it." Gil grabs the box and starts to pull it away.

Oh no. I'm definitely opening it. After all the build-up, I was taking a minute." I smile.

Carefully, I untie the silky red ribbon. Then, I lift the lid and set it on the table next to the box. There's an envelope lying on top of red tissue paper. I can't see what's under it.

"Open it and read it."

Tearing open the back, I take out a sheet of paper and a gift certificate to a local salon and spa.

My Dearest Lizzie,

I'm calling this box Unashamed Beauty. Today's going to be all about pampering you and showing you what a gorgeous woman you are—inside and out. The first order of business is a trip to the salon where you'll be treated to a Brazilian wax, massage, manicure and pedicure, hair, and make-up. After that's complete, you'll receive your next instructions.

"I don't get to open it all now?"

"Nope." He replaces the lid. "Your appointment is in a half-hour. We need to leave so you aren't late."

We get into our minivan for the ride to the salon.

"I think we should look at a new car," I suggest.

"Why? What's wrong with this one?"

"We don't need a minivan anymore."

"Can I think about it?"

"Of course."

The minivan was necessary with four kids, but now that it's only the two of us, it's perfectly reasonable to trade it in for something smaller.

Gil drops me off outside the salon.

"I'll be back in a few hours to pick you up. Enjoy yourself."

And after the torturous wax, I do exactly that. Gil thought of everything. I've never spent a day at a spa-like this, but I could easily get used to this kind of pampering.

My phone dings with a text.

(Gil) I'm here when you're ready.

He must have done a lot of planning to know exactly when I'd be finished.

When I exit the salon, Gil's waiting outside, leaning against the car. When he sees me, he stands up and meets me halfway.

"You look absolutely incredible." He kisses me, like really kisses me, in the middle of the sidewalk. "Are you ready for the next part of our date?"

"I sure am. Where are we going next?"

"Home."

I don't know what I was expecting, but I certainly didn't think we'd be going back home so soon.

Don't worry. We aren't staying there."

Me, worry?"

When we arrive home, the box is still sitting on the kitchen table.

Can I open it now?"

Go ahead."

Once again, I take the lid from the box. There's another envelope sitting on top of the tissue paper. I pick it up and open it quickly.

Lizzie,

After an afternoon of pampering, it's time to dress up for a night on the town. I can't wait to show you off. Go to our room for the next set of instructions.

It feels like I'm on a treasure hunt as I run up the steps to our bedroom. Gil follows behind but at a slower pace.

I push open the door and walk into the room. I stop and gasp when I see the long, red, satin dress hanging on the closet door. A pair of black heels are on the floor beside it. Walking over, I run my hand down the soft fabric.

Gil, this is stunning."

It'll be more stunning on you," he says, his voice deep. "I'll be in Marco's room getting changed. I'll meet you downstairs."

He leaves the bedroom, closing the door behind him.

Carefully, I slide the strapless dress off its hanger. The fabric is exquisite. It must have cost a fortune. It's clear he's put a lot of thought into this, so I try not to overthink it. I don't want to spoil his surprise. Laying the dress on the bed, I strip out of the clothes I'm wearing and then slide the dress on. Thankfully, the zipper is at the side, and I'm able to do it up on my own. Then I slide my feet into the shoes.

I can't help but walk over to the mirror. I've never worn a red dress before and am surprised to see how well it goes with my lighter skin tone and black hair.

Without dawdling, I head back downstairs to find Gil sitting on the sofa. My heels click on the wood floors alerting him to my presence.

Lizzie, you look exquisite. I have half a mind to skip the rest of the date and keep you all to myself."

Oh no, you don't," I joke. "There's still more in that box. And I'm dying to see what it is." Looking around, I don't see said box. "Where did it go?"

Where did what go?" He tilts his head and looks at me with a goofy grin.

The box."

Oh, that." He offers me his arm. "It's in the car. Let's go."

23

Gilbert

W e arrive at the restaurant right on time. I hand the valet my keys before I open Lizzie's door. She takes my offered hand, allowing me to help her out of the car. With this beautiful woman on my arm, I'm definitely the luckiest man on the earth.

The maître d greets us, "Do you have a reservation?""Yes. Benton."

He taps the screen of his tablet, scrolling down until he finds our reservation. "Please follow me."

It's early evening on Saturday, the restaurant is already packed. Heads turn, and I know they're looking at the breath-taking sight of my wife as we walk by the already seated patrons. Our table is at the back of the restaurant, where there's a row of windows overlooking the harbor. It's a beautiful view, but not more so than the woman sitting across from me.

"Gil, this place is going to cost a fortune."

We're not wealthy by any means, but we do okay for ourselves. However, this seafood restaurant is above our typical budget, but I don't care. This date is meant to indulge Lizzie. I'm hoping to show her how very special she is.

"I don't want you to worry about prices tonight. Order whatever you want." I put my hand out, and she places hers in mine. "Tonight, I'm the richest man in the world."

Often the demands of life, be it our kids, work, bills, any number of other stressors, play in my mind while I'm with Liz.

Afterward, I beat myself up for letting distractions interrupt my time with her.

Watching my children, the same ones who came into this world entirely dependent on their mom and me, grow up seemingly overnight and go off to live their own lives has been eye-opening.

Those first few years were hard. As a parent, I operated on permanent sleep deprivation and an endless supply of coffee. At the time, I didn't think those days would ever be over. But each day I woke up, the kids were bigger and bigger—and needed me less and less. I held on to Grace extra tight, trying to fool myself by pretending she'd never grow up and leave me. But, like each of her siblings before her, she did just that.

My error in all of this parenting stuff is that I refused to acknowledge the changes that were happening every day. But refusing didn't stop anyone or anything from changing. Everyone kept moving forward—everyone except me. The only thing I succeeded at was making life harder for me and those around me—especially Elizabeth.

I'm not a man who's ever coped well with change. I drove my parents crazy as a child because I insisted on routine. Any slight deviation from my schedule, and I'd meltdown.

In contrast, my brother Ryan was always easygoing and seemed to seek out change. Probably part of the reason we never got along.

When I was in my teens, my parents had had enough of my outbursts and brought me to see a psychologist. I was eventually diagnosed with high-functioning autism. My father didn't believe in therapy, so even though they had not only an explanation for my quirks, he didn't allow me to pursue the solution. I borrowed what books I could find from the library to learn as much as I could, but it's not an easy thing to cure yourself, so I eventually gave up.

Lizzie married me knowing this and is the picture of patience. Whenever possible, she gives me advanced warnings of what's coming up, which helps me tremendously, giving me time to process and prepare myself. Knowing my diagnosis made it much easier to spot the warning signs when Francesca was young. We not only pursued a diagnosis, but we also got her into the appropriate programs while she was little so that today she's fully equipped to handle challenging situations.

But for me, it still takes months to adapt to the life changes we've experienced. I had to reconcile that Grace didn't leave me. I'll always be her dad, and she'll always be my daughter. She only did what's natural, what's right.

I'm so proud of her for not allowing my resistance to change to affect her or cause her to change her plans. Grace spread her wings and is soaring, and finally, I'm able to sit back and enjoy every second of seeing her succeed on her own.

Because it's taken me so long to come around, I've lost the past few months—this precious time we should've been using to focus on each other. Instead, I was too busy moping around and refusing to change.

That's going to be different from here on out.

Putting this date box together has given me a renewed sense of purpose. With every plan I made, I felt pure joy, knowing it was all for Liz.

For dinner, we enjoy succulent lobster tails paired with creamy risotto and, per my usual, a bottle of Chardonnay. And better than the food is the conversation we share. Lizzie's eyes sparkle with excitement.

As we get closer to the end of the meal, my nerves begin to creep up. The final part of her date box will take Liz out of her comfort zone, but not because I want to see her uncomfortable. I want to show her what I see when I look at her.

After I pay the bill, we exit the restaurant. The valet is waiting with our car. I open Liz's door and help her in. Then I go around to the trunk and take the box out before getting into the drivers' seat.

"Time for the last part," I say as I hand her the box.

Liz rewards me with a beautiful smile. "Today's been incredible, Gil. I can't imagine what else there could be."

"Open it, and you'll find out."

24

Elizabeth

Today has been beyond my wildest imagination. When Gil does something, he doesn't hold back. I've been trying to figure out what else he could've planned. Maybe we're going dancing? Or to see a show?

Gil pulls the car out of the restaurant's parking lot.

With the box sitting on my lap, I lift off the lid. This time there's no envelope. Instead, there's a piece of ivory-colored stationery with a note.

My beautiful wife. When I look back over the years we've been together, I can't help but smile. I married a beautiful, spunky eighteen-year-old who has grown into a stunning and still spunky woman. Not a day goes by that I don't thank the heavens for giving you to me. Unfortunately, over the years, you've decided you aren't as beautiful as you once were—a fact I highly disagree with. Magazines, television, and society have sent the wrong message to women about what beauty is.

Tonight, I intend to set the record straight. I've chosen a few outfits, including the gorgeous red dress you're wearing, to be included in a photo shoot. My wish is when you see the photos, you'll finally see yourself as I see you. An incredibly sensual and stunning woman that I'm proud to call my wife ~Gil

By the time I finish the note, tears are streaming down my face.

"Gil, I don't know what to say."

"I know getting your picture taken isn't a favorite activity for you, but I'm hoping you'll try to keep an open mind."

"Because you planned this, I'll do my best to enjoy it." I pull the visor down and look in the lighted mirror. "Except I've ruined my make-up," she says as she looks at herself in the mirror of the visor.

"The photographer will fix it." He motions to the box. "It's time to look under the tissue paper."

When I pull the wrappings off, I'm not going to lie. I'm shocked. Inside the box is lingerie. I look over at Gil, whose eyes are fixed on the road ahead. An internal battle is waging within my soul. I'm struggling between facing my insecurities or running from the challenge. When I told Gil I would love this because he planned it, I thought there'd be some pictures in my dress and then in something casual. Lingerie never crossed my mind.

I don't know if I can do this, but I don't know how to tell him.

My hope is between here, and wherever we're going, I'll have built up the courage to at least try this photoshoot.

I recognize we're driving through Chestnut Hill, but I can't figure out where a photography studio is. This is a neighborhood, not a commercial area. Then, Gil turns onto a driveway that leads to a huge Victorian mansion.

"Is this where the photographer is?"

"Yes. She does the photoshoots out of her home." He takes my hand. "Promise me you'll try to have fun?"

"I'm not gonna lie, Gil. You shocked me with your choice of outfits." I raise my eyebrow, and he smiles. The pure joy on his face right now makes it impossible for me to back out. "I'll try to have fun."

We exit the car and walk up to the front door. He rings the bell, and a few seconds later, the door opens, and a woman stands across from us. She's young, tall, and model perfect. My instincts tell me to turn and run. That's there's no way I'm doing this with someone who looks like her.

"Hi. I'm Rory." She steps aside. "Please come in."

When we get inside, she turns to me and extends her hand.

"I'm Elizabeth. It's nice to meet you."

"It's very nice to officially meet you." Her smile is infectious. "Gilbert told me so much about you on our phone call. I feel like I already know you. Would you like to sit down, and we can talk for a little bit before we start the pictures?"

"I think that would be nice."

"Gilbert, you can wait in the living room. Feel free to watch TV while Elizabeth and I talk."

Gilbert heads into the living room while Rory and I go further down the hall. She opens the door, and we walk into a huge space. Half of it is set up as a sitting room, the other half as a bedroom. Cameras and photo equipment are scattered everywhere.

Rory takes her time explaining the photography session and everything I can expect. Her sweet demeanor helps calm my nerves some.

"Do you have any more questions, or do you want to get started?"

"Let's get started before I back out.""This'll be painless. You might even enjoy yourself." She smiles."I'm going to get Gilbert. He's not getting out of this without being in some photos."

I laugh. I don't think he realized he would be taking an active role in this.

When they return to the room, Rory turns on some music and then starts the shoot by posing us in the living room area. "Don't be afraid to move around. The best shots will be ones where you're both acting naturally. Ready?"

Without any further warning, the shutter on the camera starts clicking. Gil and I begin from a sitting position on the sofa and end up standing in each other's arms swaying to the music. After what must be a hundred pictures, Rory pauses.

"Okay, let's do a wardrobe change."

My body begins to tremble.

She looks through the lingerie in the box and pulls out a soft pink satin chemise. It's the most innocent piece Gil included. Then she points me in the direction of the changing room.

When I come out, I'm thankful to see it's just her and I.

"We're going to do some without Gil in here. Kind of a warm-up to get you more comfortable. I'll bring him back later."

"You're being so patient." I feel insecure walking around in so little clothes with the lights on. I rarely let Gil see me this much undressed unless the lights are off.

"You aren't the first woman who's come in feeling insecure and scared to death," Rory explains. "My goal is to help you relax and have fun. You're a beautiful woman, and you deserve this."

Her words give me the courage to move forward.

Rory does some shots in the sitting room before moving to the bedroom. The poses she suggests are sweet and innocent. I'm just starting to get a feel for it when she stops shooting again.

"Alright, time for the last wardrobe change."

Then she pulls out some tiny scraps of black lace. In the car, I questioned Gil about it. He insisted it was lingerie. Now Rory's insisting the same thing.

"And what part of me is this supposed to cover?"

"Take a deep breath," she says calmly. "Your husband chose this with you in mind. I know you have your doubts, but I promise. These pictures are going to be the best ones of the shoot."

"I think you're crazy." I chuckle. But I'll give it a try." I take the offered lingerie and head back into the changing room.

I was just beginning to feel comfortable in this pretty pink outfit and now I'm changing into the little bit of fabric I was given. I've never worn anything like this, and I purposely keep my back to the mirror. I'm wearing an underwire demi bra. The cups are sheer fabric with black lace edges. There's a matching thong and a lace garter belt that clips onto black thigh highs.

I'm frozen in place. I'm afraid to turn around, afraid of what I know I'll see in the mirror, and I'm equally as scared to turn the handle and leave the safety of the changing room. Without looking in the mirror, I already know my stretch marks are on full display. My breasts are droopy, and my thighs are untoned—flabby. I fight back tears. There's no way I can go out there, let alone have her take pictures of me.

"Are you okay in there?" Rory asks.

"I'm not coming out in this."

"Can you unlock the door? You don't have to come out."

Holding the pink chemise over my front, I unlock and open the door a crack.

"May I come in?"

I step aside and let Rory into the room with me.

"I can take that from you." She motions to the chemise.

I shake my head.

"I know what you're thinking."

"Please don't take this the wrong way, but how can a woman who looks like you have any idea what I'm thinking?"

"Let's sit and talk." She motions to the stools, where we both take a seat. "Liz," she says softly. "Everyone has insecurities about their body, including me."

"That's impossible. Your body is perfect."

"It's far from perfect." She chuckles. "My breasts are uneven, and I have an ugly scar on my abdomen from an emergency surgery I had several years ago. I've always wanted a thigh gap, like the models in magazines, but no matter how much I exercise,

my thighs rub together. And I also have a scar on my forehead."
She brushes her bangs aside. "I hate it, so I always have bangs,
which I hate as well."

"I don't see any of that when I look at you."

"That's my point. We're always going to be more critical of
ourselves and see things no one else will." She takes my hand and
coaxes the chemise out of it. "When Gil looks at you, he doesn't
see any of the things you feel insecure about. He only sees his
wife whom he adores."

We sit quietly for a few minutes while I think about what she's
said. I exercise and eat reasonably healthy, but nothing I do
seems to help. I've resigned myself to the fact that I'll never be
attractive again. Part of me has always thought Gil complimented
me out of some sort of obligation because he's my husband.
But would he go through all this trouble to arrange this if he
genuinely didn't find me attractive? Where I still don't see it, I
have to believe that maybe I've been wrong. Maybe he really does
think I'm pretty.

"Okay," I say softly. "Let's give it a try."

We exit the changing room and go to the bedroom area. Rory
lowers the lighting, and we do a few seductive poses on the bed.
I know she understands my insecurities when she takes a piece
of sheer black fabric and drapes it loosely over my abdomen for
some of the shots. By the time she stops shooting, I'm feeling
comfortable, almost sexy.

"Time to get Gil," she says and disappears from the room.

She returns with Gil behind her. He's wearing only his black
pants.

Thankfully, neither of them is paying attention when I wipe the
drool from my mouth. My husband doesn't think so, but I find
him super sexy. Funny, when it comes down to it, we both have
similar insecurities.

"Ready for some couple's shots?"

"Yes," Gil answers way too eagerly.

Rory has Gil sit on the bed, his legs spread so I can stand
between them, his hands on my waist. It's sexy, tasteful. Then
she starts snapping away.

"You don't have to hold the pose. Pretend I'm not here and do
what you'd naturally do."

"I don't think we want those kinds of photos," Gil jokes.

His comment makes me laugh.

Even through our banter, the click of the camera doesn't stop.

"These look amazing," she encourages us.

Gil's touch is tender as he tucks a strand of hair behind my ear. Then he rubs his knuckles gently down my cheek. I'm starting to really enjoy this. We even manage a few more steamy poses before we finish.

"I got a lot of great shots."

"Can I have a peek?" I ask.

"Nope. No peeking allowed." She chuckles. "It'll take me about a week to go through and edit them. When I'm done, I'll email a code so you can access them and place your order."

With the shoot over, I go into the changing room and put my red dress back on. When I come out, Gil's fully dressed and waiting for me.

"Thank you so much, Rory. Despite my initial hesitation, I enjoyed myself."

"That's exactly what I love to hear." She reaches out and hugs me. "I'll be in touch."

Gil and I are quiet for the first part of the drive home.

I reach out and put my hand on his leg. "Thank you for tonight."

"You don't need to thank me. It was my pleasure."

"I do. This date box was very meaningful. You put a great deal of time and thought into it, and I appreciate it."

"Liz, I'd do anything for you."

Despite my insecurities, tonight I felt sexy—still do. And once we get back to our house, I show Gil just how sexy I'm feeling.

25

Gilbert

I'm not going to lie; I was scared to death giving the Unashamed Beauty box to Liz. I wasn't sure what her reaction was going to be. Part of me feared she'd throw it back and me and tell me 'no way.' Instead, she embraced the activity, and let me just say, I don't think she's ever looked sexier.

The ride home is the longest of my life. I do the cliched Philly stop at all the intersections trying to get home as fast as possible. We barely make it inside when I pounce on her. We make it up to our bedroom this time, where I undress my wife. I lay her on the bed where I worship her body—every inch of it, including the parts she hates.

"I love you, Liz," I whisper between kisses.

Then, I slowly and gently make love to my wife.

Thankfully, it's the weekend, and we're able to sleep in because the sun was just starting to light up the night sky when we finally fell asleep.

It's a week to the day when I receive an email from Rory with the code for our pictures. Liz is out to lunch with Kelly, and although I'm tempted to look at them, I promised her we'd do it together.

I busy myself with some work on the cedar chest for Marco and Ivy. It's almost finished, and I think it's some of the best work I've done so far. I'm supposed to be sanding the wood and getting it prepped for stain, but I'm having a hard time focusing. I find myself obsessively checking the time. But each time I look, barely a minute has passed. Is time at a standstill?

My willpower is slipping away, and I consider texting Liz begging her to come home early, but I won't interrupt her time with Kelly.

With my mind racing in a million directions, I'm finding concentration to be next to impossible. Since I don't want to screw up the piece of furniture, so I come back upstairs and decide to run the vacuum and do some laundry—anything to keep myself busy.

Finally, I hear them pull up. Hurrying to the door, I have it open before Liz is even out of the car.

"Did you miss me that much?" Liz jokes as she comes into the house.

"Well, yes." I kiss her. "I have a surprise for you."

"A surprise?" Liz's eyes open wide.

"The pictures are ready."

The smile she had just a second ago is now gone, replaced by a look for uncertainty. "I guess you want to look at them." Her voice is shaky.

"I do." I take her hand, leading her to the kitchen where I left my laptop.

We, our chairs close together, so we can both see the screen. I pull up Rory's website and type in the passcode. With the click of a button, my screen fills with images of Liz, both alone and of us as a couple. Slowly, I scroll through them, transfixed by the images on my screen.

Most of the photos are in color, but I find the black and white ones most striking. Looking at these pictures, one would never know the woman being photographed was insecure. She owned every outfit and every pose. Liz looks sexy—exquisite.

The pictures of us together have somehow captured not only our image, but our emotions and personality. Whether the shot is one of the poses or one of the more candid moments, I think they're all perfect.

When we get to the end, I turn and look at Liz. She hasn't said anything the entire time. Instead, she's biting her lips and squeezing her hands together so hard her knuckles are turning white.

"What's wrong? Don't you like them?"

Great job, Gil. You've really screwed this up.

It takes her a minute to answer. "When I look at pictures of myself, the only things I usually notice are all my flaws. I never see anything remotely pretty. But these." She points at the screen. "They're incredible. They make me feel pretty."

"This's exactly what I was hoping for." I put my arm around her and pull her close to me. "I want you to look at yourself and know how gorgeous you are."

We did our best to pick our favorite shots, but we end up ordering almost every picture Rory took. Most of them will remain private, for Liz and my eyes only. But we did find a few that we'll hang on our wall.

Not only do I get to show off my sexy wife, but on those days where she's inevitably going to struggle with her body image, she can look at her pictures and remember how she's feeling right now.

Since this date was so successful, we decided to have a pre-order for an Unashamed Beauty Date Box. Keeping in mind that not everyone will be local, we tweaked the box, so it's an in-house activity that can be done with a cell phone camera.

I've designed the box to mimic my setup. There are three pieces of stationery for one partner to write notes, just like I did, to guide the other partner through the date. We also include a string of LED lights, and three pieces of lingerie ranging from sweet and innocent to hot and spicy. We made a suggested playlist for during the shoot. And lastly, a decorative photo album for any pictures the couple may want to have in print. It's been listed for less than a week, and we already have over 100 orders.

I'll admit, I'm shocked at the amount of interest we have this soon.

We make a list of date ideas to try out over the next few weekends. They'll be both in-home and out on the town options. Our goal is to have a large enough selection of dates to attract as many couples as possible. I think we're compiling a good list of playful, sweet, sexy, daring, sensual, themed, bondage, and costumed. We want to make sure there's as much variety as possible for everyone's comfort level.

Eventually, I'd like to offer a custom fantasy box. My idea is the customer would tell us their fantasy ahead of time. We'll have some general safety guidelines in place. Our job will be to compile everything needed to bring their fantasy to life.

Liz's idea for bringing Real Life Romance to fruition has been nothing but successful. We've been spending a lot of time together, not only planning the dates but also trying them out. It's exactly what we'd planned for this point in our lives—minus running a website.

If everything is going so well, then why am I having doubts? Shouldn't I be happy to do all these exciting things with my wife? Yes, and I'm glad we're spending time together. But shouldn't a date be about focusing on one another? Spending quality time together? What I'm seeing is the more dates we plan, the more they feel like business meetings. Rather than having conversations with each other, our heads are down while we each take notes and compile supply lists. When we get home, instead of continuing the date, we're comparing notes.

I'm beginning to fear this newfound connection isn't real—it's only because of the website.

26

Elizabeth

Tribe friends, I can't believe how much fun we're having with RealLifeRomance.org. The list of do-it-yourself dates has grown. We've had tremendous success with the first pre-made date box and are planning to add a few more to the list. Orders are coming in by the dozen every day.

This is exactly what Gil and I needed. I feel like we're newlyweds again—or maybe for the first time since we really didn't get much time alone during our newlywed days. All week I look forward to the weekend and what new date idea we're going to try.

Keep throwing those suggestions at us!

On another note, summer is approaching quickly, which means the end of Grace's first year of college. We were looking forward to her coming home for the summer holiday, especially since we haven't seen her since she left in August. But even the best-laid plans fall through. She's coming to Philly, but only for a week. The conservation center has a small group of employees who rotate shifts—Grace is one of them. She doesn't feel it's right for her to blow off her job for an entire summer. I'm a bit disappointed, who wouldn't be? But I'm also very proud of the responsible young woman she is.

Did you happen to notice I didn't say Grace was coming home? There's twist number two. Instead of staying with us, Grace's staying at a friend's home while she's in town. I get it. She's grown accustomed to her independence and doesn't want to stay with mom and dad.

How did Gil handle this news, you ask? He's taken up walking—long-distance walking. Does that help answer the question? In true Grace fashion, she gave no hints that her summer plans would be different than we initially thought. It took him some time and about ten miles to adjust.

On a positive note, he's mentioned that maybe we should take a trip out there to visit her. Hawaii is supposed to be our 30th wedding anniversary trip, but if we can go sooner, I'm all for it.

And for those that asked about the photoshoot and if I'll post the pictures. Yes, I'll post a few of them, but most are for our eyes only. A few of you have asked for information on the photographer. I'll post Rory's information below. Tell her I sent you. ~Lizzie

I hit publish, then sit back in my chair and blow out a big breath. Overwhelmed is an excellent way to describe how I'm feeling. Between blogging and Real Life Romance, there's a lot of work. The website took off a lot faster than either of us ever imagined.

While Gil's at work, I'm busy talking with our suppliers and ordering product so we can fill the orders that are piling up. As the shipments come in, I inventory and organize everything. At night, when Gil's home, we try to fill as many orders as possible before we're exhausted and we collapse in bed. The next day, I make sure the packed orders get shipped and start the cycle all over again.

I'm in way over my head.

Before I crack, I need to lighten my load so I can focus my time and energy in one place. As difficult as it will be, I'm considering ending my blog. Just thinking about it makes me sad. "Finding my Tribe" has been a big part of my life for so many years. While the kids were young and we were fully engulfed with homeschooling, the blog was my lifeline to the outside world. My readers became my second family. But now, that chapter feels like it's closing, and I'm moving in a new direction. That's a decision I'll have to make soon, but right now, the time on my cell phone lets me know I need to start dinner.

With us being so busy with orders, we've been either getting takeout or microwaving frozen food. Both of which get old fast. A few weeks ago, we found Fresh Express, one of those weekly meal delivery services. We decided to give it a try and quickly fell in love. It's perfect, we pick our meals for the week, and they're delivered to our doorstep. All I have to do is take the bag out of my fridge. All the ingredients are neatly packaged, and there's even a recipe card with super easy instructions. My only regret is that we didn't do this years ago. It's made cooking feel like less of a chore.

Everything is going great until my phone pings.

(Gil) I'm sorry to do this, but I'm going to be late tonight.

(Liz) Don't tell me, Camila?

(Gil) Yes. She made a huge error. We have to get it fixed tonight, or Chris's inspections will expire. He'll have to start the process all over. It'll put him way behind.

Gil's best friend Chris owns a contracting business and, much like my husband, is on a mission to provide safe, clean, and affordable housing for the citizens of Philadelphia. Last year he bought several blocks of rundown rowhouses. He has a plan that will revolutionize the area and could be easily replicated in some of the city's other neighborhoods.

I've seen his digital blueprints. His ideas are unlike anything that's ever been attempted. Chris doesn't only want to modernize the housing; he's also secured grants to add playgrounds and community garden spaces. His goal is to attract young families to create a flourishing neighborhood. Gil has been on board from day one and is doing everything to keep the project moving.

Surprise, surprise, Camila strikes again. I have a sneaking suspicion she's making these mistakes on purpose, but without any proof, my hands are tied. Things are good between Gil and me right now. I don't want to upset the apple cart by having another argument about her.

(Liz) It's not a problem. I didn't put dinner on yet. Text me when you're on your way so I can start cooking.

(Gil) Thanks. You're the best.

With some extra time on my hands, I decide to run myself a nice hot bubble bath. It'll give me a chance to close my eyes and relax, rather than hyper-focusing on the thought that Gil is alone with that woman.

27

Gilbert

I hate upsetting Lizzie, and I know I did. But I have no other choice. This is the most significant error Camila's made yet. If it doesn't get fixed, Chris's project will face severe delays, which means more money for him. I won't allow that because of an issue in my department.

"I'm so sorry about this mess," Camila says for the millionth time. "I don't know how it went this wrong."

"I don't know either." I try to mask my growing frustration.

She sighs dramatically. "And now we're stuck here late, again." Then, she stands up and makes a show of stretching.

Out of the corner of my eye, I see her blouse ride up, exposing her abdomen. She holds the pose a second too long and looks at me with a smile. Is she hoping to get some kind of reaction? If she is, she will be sorely disappointed because she doesn't get one.

"I think we should order dinner." She picks up her phone. "What are you hungry for?"

"Camila, please sit down and finish the paperwork." I motion to the pile of papers in front of her. "We need to stay focused on fixing all this, get it properly filed, and then we can go home."

"I didn't mean to upset you." She sits back down and crosses her leg. "It's getting late. I thought you might be getting hungry."

"It is, and I am." I lift my head. "I have dinner waiting at home for me."

Without any further argument, Camila gets back to work.

Although she's been with our office for a little over a year, she's only been doing permit jobs for the past four or five months. As frustrating as this is, I have to remember this is still new to her. I've gotten used to working with the others who've been with the department for years and don't make these kinds of potentially costly errors. The hard part is Camila is one of only a small number of females in this department, so I feel like I have to tread carefully. I don't want any reprimands to come off as harassment or discrimination. However, if things don't start improving, I'll be forced to speak to my superiors.

Nearly three hours later, we're filing the last of the paperwork online. I'm exhausted, but it's done before the midnight deadline. Once I get the online confirmation, I call Chris, who answers on the first ring.

"Did you get it done?" he asks, his voice panicked.

"Just finished uploading everything. I'll email you the confirmation number."

"Thank you, Gil. I owe you for this."

"It's my job. I just wish it had been done correctly the first time."

"I have to ask. What's with that girl? I got a bad vibe when she was here."

"What do you mean?"

"She wouldn't stop talking about you," he says. "How close the two of you work and how she loves spending time with you in the office. It was odd."

Why would she be talking about me on a job? That's not exactly professional. It's probably because I told her Chris was a good friend of mine, but it's still not okay. I make a note to remind everyone in the office about our professional standards.

But a bad vibe? Chris knows Liz doesn't like her, so that's probably it. He's like a brother to me and is fiercely protective of both Liz and me. If he knows Liz doesn't like someone, there's no way Chris will like them.

"Are you sure she didn't do it on purpose? Liz said—"

"She didn't do it on purpose." I cut him off. "She's still learning."

"If you say so, but I'd be careful if I were you."

"I'll keep that in mind."

We say our goodbyes, and I shut down my system.

"Let's go," I hold the door open for Camila and then lock up.

We walk out together, and as usual, when it's dark, I walk her to her car. Why? Because it's the right thing to do.

When we get to her car, she reaches out and takes my hand. "Thank you for being so patient with me."

"It was an honest mistake."

"I do like spending the time with you." She rubs circles on my hand with her thumb. "There's so much I can learn from you."

I shrug out of her touch. "Get in your car, Camila."

She flashes a smile. "Goodnight, Gilbert."

"Night." I turn and quickly walk to my car, where I text Liz.

(Gil) I'm just pulling out now. See you soon.

(Liz) Must've been a lot of paperwork.

(Gil) It was, but we got it in on time. That's all that matters.

(Liz) Yep. That's all that matters.

I'm too tired to have a text argument, so I toss the phone onto the passenger seat and start the drive home. Thankfully, there's not a lot of traffic at this time of the evening. It only takes twenty minutes before I'm home.

When I walk in, Liz is in the kitchen. I smell dinner cooking.

"Hi, honey." I kiss her cheek. "I'm sorry."

"Mhm."

I empty my lunch bag, rinse the containers, and put them in the dishwasher.

"I had no choice, Liz. The paperwork had to get in before midnight."

"I know." She turns away to put a tray of potato wedges in the oven.

"So, that's it. I'm only going to get one- or two-word answers?"

"Mhm." She starts setting the table.

I'm exhausted, and now I'm frustrated with my wife. Does she think I enjoy staying late? That I wouldn't have preferred to come home on time? If I stay in the room any longer, we're going to end up fighting, and I don't like arguing with Liz.

"I'm going to go take a quick shower before dinner."

I get no response, so I leave the room to take a long, hot shower. Hopefully, that'll wash off the frustration of the day and give Liz some time to get herself together.

28

Elizabeth

G il strolled in at almost eleven o'clock. He acted like I should be happy, maybe do a few cartwheels because he finally came home.

I. Don't. Think. So.

Now he's complaining that I'm only giving him one-or-two-word answers. If I say any more than that, I'm going to explode, and trust me, he doesn't want that—I don't want that.

I just want to have a quiet meal, go to bed, and pretend tonight never happened.

I'm taking dinner out of the oven just as Gil comes downstairs.

"It smells wonderful. I'm starving."

"Me too."

"Liz." He takes my hand. "I'm sorry about tonight. I had to get that stuff done."

"I know. But that doesn't make it any easier when I'm here, and I know you're alone at the office all night with Camila."

"What does that mean?" Where is she going with this?

"I think you know what I'm talking about."

"Nothing is going on between us."

"I trust you, Gil. It's her that's the problem. Can't you see that?""I guess." He shrugs.

"You guess?""I know she's said some hurtful things, and that's not okay, but she's harmless. She's a young girl trying to get attention."

Oh, my sweet, innocent husband.

From the time we were teenagers and started dating, he could never see when a girl was after him or flirted with him. He says it's because he only has eyes for me.

It never used to bother me. I'd simply laugh it off and move on. Maybe it was because I was more confident in my looks back then. I knew I could compete with any of the other girls who were desperately trying to get his attention.

But now, now I am washed up. Expired, as Camila put it. This stretched-out, saggy body can't compete against someone like Camila. Although I trust Gilbert, he's only human. What if she makes an advance when he's not expecting it? What if he decides I'm not what he wants anymore? What if? What if? What if? I'm going to drive myself crazy with all the what-ifs.

"Can we change the subject?" I ask as I set the food on the table, and we take our seats.

"Did our inventory come today?"

"It did. It's in the office."

"How many orders do we have left to pack?""There's fifty we had left, and we got another twenty-five today."

"That's incredible." He makes his plate. "When you first brought up this idea, I really didn't think it would catch on. I guess I was wrong."

I make my plate and take a bite of the chicken. "I knew it would eventually catch on, but I'm surprised it happened so fast."

"I'm sure it's partly because you already have an online presence," he says between bites.

"I'm thinking of giving up the blog."

"Why? You love blogging."

"I do, but I'm struggling with a lack of time."

I explain how much fun I'm having with the new website, not to mention how good the boost in income has been.

"It's time-consuming. I'm not complaining, but I need to find a better balance, and when I put everything on the table, the blog is the thing that needs to go."

"I'll support you whatever you decide."

And there's my wonderful husband again. He supports me in everything. I have to figure out a way to put this disdain for Camila away. If I don't, I fear it may be me and my attitude that drives him into her arms.

Like it or not, she's his co-worker. But I have a big advantage—I'm his wife.

29

Gilbert

It was a long week at work, which is why I'm looking forward to going out with Liz tonight. This date has been planned for several weeks.

One of the local culinary schools has a community outreach program. Once a month, for a nominal fee, they host cooking classes. Liz and I signed up for this one weeks ago. We're going to be making homemade pasta carbonara. Yes, Liz is already an expert pasta maker, but I am not. And for dessert, we'll be making chocolate truffles.

We walk into the school's kitchen and there are already three other couples there.

"Welcome. I'm Chef Marc." The energetic instructor greets us.

"Hi. I'm Gilbert. This is my wife, Elizabeth."

After the introductions, we're each given an apron and shown to our assigned station.

Two more couples join before Chef Marc gets started.

"First, we're going to work on our pasta," he explains. "Take your flour and make a well on the counter."

Liz is taking a back seat on this part. She's been making pasta since she was a little girl. I watch Chef Marc's demonstration closely and decide this should be a piece of cake.

Carefully, I empty the flour and make a hole in the center. I crack the first egg, no problem. Second egg—still good. Third egg—things start to fall apart. Part of my well splits, and egg seeps onto the counter.

Working quickly, I shift the flour in an attempt to rebuild the dam, but that only makes it worse. Other areas of what I thought was my leak proof well begin to give way. Egg is now seeping through at a rate too fast for me to fix.

"What do I do?" I'm hoping Liz can bail me out. When I look up, instead of finding my rescue coming, she's giggling away while she's filming the whole episode. "You're taping this?" My hands, which are covered in a sloppy egg and flour mess, are currently acting as makeshift walls.

"You bet." She slides the phone into her pocket.

Before she's able to step in, Chef Marc walks by. "And what have we got going on here?"

"I think I did something wrong." Egg has now crept under my hands and is dripping from the counter to the floor. Our classmates are whispering and giggling. I'm glad they're getting a laugh at my expense.

"Let me give you a hand," Liz says and steps in beside me.

Somehow, she works her magic and quickly incorporates whatever is left of the egg into the flour. The mess now becomes a proper dough ball.

"I can get it from here," I say, desperate to prove to my wife that I can do this.

Thankfully, the rest of the process goes much smoother, and we have long strands of homemade pasta hanging on a drying rack waiting to be cooked.

"We're going to get our dessert prepped and in the blast freezer." He points to the appliance at the other end of the kitchen. "Otherwise, we'd have to wait a few hours for them to cool."

"First, you need to chop the chocolate into fine pieces," Liz reads the directions. "While you do that, I'll heat the heavy cream."

"Okay." I should be able to do this with no problems.

I finish cutting the chocolate just in time. Lizzie is just coming back with the heated cream.

"What's next?" I ask.

"I need to mix the butter in with the cream. Then it gets poured over the chocolate."

Liz stirs the butter into the cream while I scrape the chocolate from the cutting board into the shallow dish we were given.

"I'll pour it," I offer.

I tip the pot slowly so I don't splash the liquid out of the dish. Chef Marc chooses this moment to walk by our station. I only look up for a second, and it happens. The dish with the chocolate and cream starts to slip. Liz goes to grab it, but I get it first. Instead of righting the dish, it flips. The liquidy chocolate mixture flies from the dish and lands all over Liz.

She shrieks.

I drop the pot with a clang. "Are you burned?"

"No, I'm okay." She looks at me, her eyes wide. "I'm just covered in chocolate."

There's splashes of chocolate dotting her face. Her shirt is covered.

"I'm sorry." I reach for the hand towel hanging on our station and try to wipe her off, but it only spreads the chocolate around. "I've ruined your shirt."

Looking around, everyone in the kitchen has stopped what they're doing and is now staring at us.

"It's okay. It'll wash out." Liz is handling this much better than me.

Chef Marc has brought over several more towels. Liz tries to soak up as much of the chocolate as possible, but it isn't working. The more she wipes, the worse it gets.

"I think we're going to need to leave early," Liz says apologetically.

"Of course. I wipe my hands on one of the towels. I'm sorry I ruined our date."

Liz smiles. "You haven't ruined anything."

I want to cry. This was supposed to be fun. We were supposed to cook the food we prepped and then sit down for a nice dinner, but now we have to walk out right in the middle of the class.

"Let me package your pasta and the rest of the stuff for your carbonara," Chef Marc offers.

"Thank you. We appreciate that." Liz is gracious, even as she's covered in what was supposed to be our dessert.

"Let me wipe your face." Liz turns to me, and I do my best to wipe the chocolate splatters from her nose and cheeks.

She licks her lip, getting the chocolate off. "Yum. It tastes delicious."

Chef Marc returns with a paper bag containing our dinner. "Here you go." He hands it to me. "I hope the two of you come back and give this another try."

I nod out of politeness. However, I don't think I'll ever be able to show my face in here again.

Liz handles it all with grace. Once we get outside, she starts laughing. I freeze on the sidewalk and watch my wife as she nearly doubles over with laughter.

"What's so funny?""This." She motions to her shirt.

"It's anything but funny."

"Look at me. I'm covered in chocolate," she says.

It's unavoidable to do anything but see the chocolate all over her. She pulls her cell phone out.

"Come here, let's take a selfie."

"Are you kidding?"

"No," she says. "This is one date I'll never forget, and I want a picture to show for it."

She holds the phone up, ready to snap the picture. That's when I realize she's serious. Despite my reservations, I stand next to her.

"Smile."

"I don't want to."

"I'm the one wearing dessert. I think I earned the write to tell you to smile."

I can't argue with her, so I put a smile on my face. Liz snaps a few pictures.

"When we get to the car, I'm going to send this to the kids."

I storm off in the direction of her car. The sooner we get out of here, the better.

"It's okay to laugh, Gil," she calls.

"Laugh?" I spin around.

"Yes, laugh."

My wife is standing in the middle of the parking lot, covered in chocolate, with a huge smile on her face. There's no hint of anger or frustration visible. I walk back in her direction and don't stop until our bodies touch each other. The chocolate is now smudged on my T-shirt. I do the only thing I can at this moment. I kiss her.

"You taste like chocolate." I pull back. "I couldn't let you have all the fun." I wink at my wife, and we both share a laugh.

This date might just end up in my top ten. Liz could've freaked out, but she didn't. She laughed—we laughed.

And the best part. We didn't take a single note for the website.

30

Elizabeth

It's early May, but it's been warm all week, and I have a wicked case of Spring fever. My plan for the day is to get outside to start prepping the garden, but first, I have something to do.

Firing my laptop up, I log into my blog page to pen my farewell post.

Fellow tribes people—friends. Today I come to you with some bittersweet news. This will be my farewell post to Finding my Tribe. We've been together for so many years and have seen each other through both ups and downs, so this is a difficult step to take.

You all know Gil, and I started a new endeavor with RealLifeRomance.org. What began as a pipe dream has quickly turned into a full-time job. We're receiving so many orders. A huge thank you to all of you who are ordering. I'm finding there aren't enough hours in the day. I've been struggling with keeping up with the website, my personal life, and the blog. After a great deal of soul-searching and a lot of tears, I've decided to shut down Finding My Tribe.

So, a last update on life with the Benton's. It seems like only yesterday we were dealing with sleepless nights, loose teeth, and schoolwork. In the middle of the chaos of homeschooling four children, there were times I didn't think it would ever end or if I would survive. Let me tell you, when four little people gang up on you, it's a terrifying moment!!

One by one, those little people grew up. Each one in their own time took their first adult steps out into the world to trailblaze their own path. And they are all doing so well. Each day they amaze me with their confidence and success. I'm thankful to have had a part in shaping each of them.

Want a juicy tidbit? Ryker, Francesca's boyfriend, called and asked if he could come over tonight to talk to us. I have a sneaking suspicion our daughter will be getting engaged very soon.

Gil and I are finally living the empty nest life we dreamed of. Over the past several months, we've had many date adventures—some more successful than others. We're finally embracing our lives as a couple. We've always been in love, but during those child-raising days, our priority was always our kids. Fanning the flames of romance took a back burner to being parents. Their needs came before ours, sometimes to a fault. But in the end, everything's worked out.

Embarking on the journey of starting Real Life Romance has been one of the best things we've done.

So, my friends, I leave you with this.

I encourage each and every one of you to live every day to the fullest. Don't be afraid to dance in the rain. Take chances. Make sure to laugh, even if it's at yourself. Take your bucket list and do everything on it—have no regrets.

Find your tribe and love them hard—that was my motto when I wrote my first post all those years ago. I found you, and I love you all very much. This isn't goodbye, this is see you later.

Love you all always ~Lizzie

I click send on my final post.

Sitting back in my chair, tears pour down my face as I allow myself to feel the emotions of the moment. Finding my Tribe has been a part of my life for over ten years. As necessary as this step is, I'm already feeling the loss. But I know, as with all things, time will heal this wound.

I'm thankful when Ryker texts to let me know he's bringing dinner with him. I decided to day would be a self-care day.

I've been wanting to take up yoga, so I searched Amazon for a beginner video. It actually wasn't too bad. I found the flute music nearly hypnotic, and the movements were relaxing. Relaxing and exercise in the same sentence that's actually kinda comical, but it's the truth. I'm sure I wasn't anywhere near as graceful as the woman teaching the video class, but I'm not opposed to doing it again.

I'm just getting out of the shower when I hear Gil's car pull up. Did I take that long? I rush to the clock in the bedroom and see it's only 4:00.

I'm still wrapped in my towel when I walk to the top of the steps. I wait until I hear the door open and close before I call, "What are you doing home already?"

"I couldn't concentrate on work, so I decided to leave early." He walks upstairs and kisses my cheek. "How was your afternoon?"

A lump forms in my throat when I try to answer him. "It's been a tough day."

Gil opens his arms, and I fall into him.

"Don't cry." He kisses the top of my head. "It's going to be an adjustment, but you'll be okay."

"Says the man who runs from change."

"It makes for good advice, though." He chuckles. "You should go get dressed."

Gil sits in the bedroom while I dry my hair and get ready.

"We should check on the website before Ryker gets here," I call from the bathroom where I'm putting some make-up on.

"It can wait until tomorrow."

I poke my head around the door. "If I don't print off today's orders, I'm liable to be inundated tomorrow."

"I think we should come up with some business hours."

I go back to the mirror to finish applying my lipstick. "Business hours? We don't need business hours. It's not like we're interacting one-on-one with customers."

"I don't want to see the website overshadow everything else."

With my make-up finished, I return to the bedroom. "Since we're the trial and error for the site, I don't think there's much separation between our lives and our business."

31

Gilbert

'I don't think there's much separation between our lives and our business.' Liz's words are exactly what I feared was happening. Every date we have, everything we do is less about us and more about the website.

Unfortunately, the doorbell interrupts our conversation, but it's something we're going to have to come back to. It feels like whenever we have any semblance of free time, Liz has us in the office working. I know we have a lot of orders, but we can't sacrifice our private lives for the website. We need to find a balance.

We head downstairs to answer the door. When I open it, Ryker's on the other side holding two boxes of pizza.

"Mr. Benton, you're home early," Ryker says.

"You're early too." I step aside to let him in.

"I know. I'm sorry." He walks into the kitchen and sets the boxes on the table. "I've been driving around for the past hour trying to kill time."

I mask my laugh with a cough. "I'm glad you got here early. I didn't have time to take a lunch today, so I'm starving." I catch Lizzie's eye over his shoulder, and she smiles.

"That's good then, sir." Ryker stumbles over his words.

"Ryker, breathe."

"Breathe. Right." His shoulders rise as he takes a deep breath.

Liz grabs some paper plates and napkins. "Have a seat, Ry."

"Yes, ma'am."

I take the plates and napkins from Liz. She goes to the fridge and grabs a few cans of soda before returning. The three of us sit at the table and make our plates.

Liz and I start eating, but Ryker just plays with his napkin.

I set my slice of pizza on the plate. "I'm pretty certain you didn't come here just to have dinner with us."

"I don't mind having dinner with you," Ryker says quickly.

"That's not what I mean, son."

"Oh yeah." He wrings his hands nervously. "There's something I want to talk to you about."

"Okay." I fold my hands in front of me.

"Francesca and I have been dating for three years now."

He doesn't need to remind me of that. Even though she was homeschooled, the law allowed her to participate in the sports offered by our school district. Frannie ran cross country in the fall and track and field in the spring.

It was her senior year of high school when she met Ryker at a track meet. Her school used the fields at Drexel University, where Ryker was a senior. They hit it off right away. Even though Francesca was eighteen, I was concerned about their age difference. Ryker came to the house frequently for dinner and to hang out, but I didn't allow them to formally date for nearly a year.

I liked the kid, but secretly, I hoped he'd get bored and go away. I wasn't ready to let go of my firstborn daughter.

But he didn't get bored, and he didn't go away.

He stayed and earned my trust. They've been together ever since.

"Yes, you have," I say coolly.

"Well, Um. I love her very much."

"I'm glad to hear that."

"And, well, I'd like to ask you permission for something."

His entire body is trembling in fear. However, I don't give an inch. I know what he's planning on asking, but I'm going to make him work for it.

"And what is it you'd like to ask?"

Ryker looks back and forth between Liz and me. "I'd like to ask your permission to marry Francesca."

I don't move or react for several drawn-out minutes. When Ryker called this morning, I knew exactly what was going to happen tonight, and I've spent the entire day trying to decide how to handle it. I settle on taking the approach Liz's dad took with me when I asked his permission to marry Liz.

I remember it well. It was the day before our high school graduation and it was unusually hot for the beginning of June. Marco suggested we head over to Valley Forge to "take advantage of the weather." There were no clouds in the sky. The sun beat down on us as we walked through the historical battlegrounds. Sweat dripped from every part of my body, but Marco looked calm and relaxed. We must've walked five or six miles in silence before I worked up the courage to speak.

When I finally got the question out, Marco said, "Gilbert, we could've been back in the air conditioning if you asked five miles ago."

"Why didn't you stop walking?" I asked him. "I wasn't letting you off the hook that easy. If you want my blessing to marry my daughter, you have to work for it."

We found a nearby bench that thankfully was in the shade, where we sat and talked. Although Marco and I had a good relationship, this conversation was serious. He was stern and didn't give an inch. He wanted to know how I planned to support his daughter. Where we would live. How soon I was thinking about having this wedding, among many other questions. I was shaking in my Asics while I tried to answer each one as thoroughly as possible, knowing I was an eighteen-year-old kid with little to offer.

One of my dad's friends worked in the housing authority office and was able to get me an afterschool job there. I did any and all of the odd tasks that needed to be done—filing, shredding, and even emptying wastepaper baskets if asked. The salary wasn't much, but it was a regular paycheck.

I'd already accepted a scholarship offer from Temple University to study Business Management. My goal was to get a real job at the housing authority. As for where we'd live, well, we hadn't figured that much out yet. We ended up in a tiny, one-bedroom apartment in South Philly.

It wasn't much, but it was ours.

So, like my father-in-law before me, I took Ryker for a walk around the neighborhood. This time it's my turn as the father-in-law-to-be.

"How do you plan to support my daughter?"

Ryker's complexion is nearly see-through. I'm afraid he may pass out.

"I'm going to be starting a new job in the fall."

"You are?" This is the first I'm hearing about this new development.

"Yes." He smiles for the first time since he came over. "I'm going to be teaching first grade at Kingston Elementary."

Ryker works in the district's after-school childcare program and has been a substitute for several years. Getting a full-time position has been his goal for some time now. He's passionate about working with children, and from what I hear, they respond great to him. I'm thrilled that he's finally seeing his dreams come true.

"That's great, Ry. Congratulations." I pat his shoulder. "I'm assuming that means you and Francesca will be remaining in New Jersey?

"Yes, sir. We're looking at purchasing a home there."

Seems there's lots of news my daughter and her soon-to-be fiancé have been keeping to themselves.

"Oh?"

"We've been holding off on telling anyone until we were certain it was a done deal. We put a bid on a house, and it was accepted." He pulls his cell out. "Would you like to see the pictures?""Sure."

The house is an older, fully renovated colonial-style home with three bedrooms. Knowing how much Francesca loves to cook, I'm particularly interested in the kitchen, which is huge. It's modern with white cabinets and dark grey granite countertops.

"I'm sure Frannie loves this kitchen."

"She does. It's honestly what sold us on this house over some others we looked at."

I continue scrolling through the pictures. The bedrooms are all a neutral, light grey, and have hardwood floors.

"I know how difficult change is for Francesca, so we wanted to make sure the house is affordable but big enough to meet our long-term needs," Ryker explains.

"Do you and she plan on having children?"

"Yes, sir." He nods. "We aren't sure when, but we want to have a family."

I'm glad to hear that there's the hope of grandkids in the future. It'll be nice to have babies around again, but this time we have the option of sending them home at the end of the day.

We've been walking for so long the sun is starting to set, and the air is turning chilly. I guess it's time to let the boy off the hook. Making a right at the corner, we head back toward the house.

"Liz and I would be pleased to have you as our son-in-law."

"You would?" His voice raises an octave.

"Of course." I laugh. "You two have been together a long time, and I know how much you love each other." I stop walking. "Marriage is a serious commitment, one that takes constant work from both of you. You two are going to have disagreements and the occasional fight. My advice." I start walking again. "Is never go to bed angry. Even if that means staying up all night to find your resolution. That's something my father-in-law told me when I asked to marry Liz, and it's the advice that's helped the most."

"I'll remember that," Ryker assures me.

"When are you planning to ask her?"

"We're going to Cape May in two weeks. I'm going to ask her while we're there."

"Good luck, son. Although I don't think you're going to need it." For the first time since he arrived, he takes a deep breath. The color returns to his face.

"Thanks, Mr. Benton." He stops mid-step. "What am I supposed to call you now?"

"Like I've told you for a long time, Gil is fine."

"I was wondering." He finishes walking up the few steps to our porch. "Would I be able to call you dad?"

This time I'm stunned silent.

Ryker's mom passed away from cancer when he was barely three years old. He has no memory of her. His dad raised him but never remarried. Shortly after Ryker and Francesca started dating, he and his dad were in a terrible car accident. Ryker got out with only a broken arm and several broken ribs, but his father didn't make it. Ryker was devastated.

My eyes fill with tears, and I struggle to get my words out. "I'd be very honored by that, son."

Ryker loses the battle to tears. I put my hand on his shoulder in an attempt to console him.

"Thank you, dad," he says quietly. "It feels good to have a father again." Ryker turns and hugs me.

That's about all I can handle before the dam breaks, and I cry with him.

32

Elizabeth

G il and Ryker have been gone for quite a while. I hope he isn't giving Ryker a hard time. The poor kid was so nervous.

I open the front door intending to look if they're on their way back yet, and am surprised to see them on the porch. Both of them are in tears.

When they notice me, they jump back from their embrace and try to wipe their eyes discreetly.

"I'm sorry. I didn't know you two were out here." I feel bad for interrupting whatever moment they were having.

"It's okay." Gil kisses my cheek as he walks past me. "We were just on our way in."

"I have a question to ask you too, Mrs. Benton."

"What is it?"

"If Francesca says yes, would you be okay if I call you mom?" The reason for their tears is apparent, and now I'm crying too. I grab Ryker and squeeze him tight. "I'd love that."

Ryker stays for a cup of coffee and tells us his plans for the proposal.

"I'm going to wait until sunset and I'll ask her on the beach. Afterward, I have reservations at one of our favorite restaurants."

By the time he's done, I'm swooning. The boy is a true romantic.

"Thank you for letting me come by," Ryker says. "I wasn't sure how you were going to respond, Mr., I mean dad."

"I'll be proud to call you my son."

I walk Ryker out and wait until he drives off before I go back inside, where I find Gil sitting on the couch, his head back.

"Are you okay?"

"I think so," he says.

I sit next to him and snuggle close to his side. He wraps his arm around me.

"I knew the question was coming, but it was still hard to say yes. I'm turning over the care and protection of my daughter to him."

"Ryker's a good man. Francesca chose well." "She did," he agrees. "But Gracie better not get any ideas. I'm not ready for that again."

I laugh. "That day will come soon enough."

"Do you know something I don't?" In fact, I do, but she asked me not to say anything.

Grace met someone in Hawaii. She sent me his picture. He's a handsome young man, a native Hawaiian, named Makoa. He's coming home with Grace in two weeks two meet us. But tonight is not the time to drop that bomb on Gil.

"I know it's late, and I'd like it if you'd take me to bed."

Gil squints his eyes, scrutinizing me. "Is this a diversion tactic?"

"Maybe," I giggle. "Is it working?"

"Maybe."

Two weeks fly by, and we're driving to the airport. Grace's plane is scheduled to land in a little under an hour.

"Grace has a bit of a surprise for you." It's time to let the proverbial cat out of the bag.

"Oh?" He glances at me quickly before returning his eyes to the road. "As long as she's not bringing a boy home, we're good."

Gulp. We might be in trouble.

"And if it is a boy?" I ask hesitantly.

"Don't even joke about that, Liz." He shakes his head.

"I'm not joking. Grace met someone a few months ago."

"Why didn't she tell me?"

She didn't even mean to tell me. I only found out because Grace accidentally texted me instead of Frannie. My phone rang seconds after I responded to her text, a panicked Grace on the other end.

"I didn't mean to text you, Mom. Please don't say anything to dad."

"Why not?" I asked

"Mom," she said, drawing out the letter sounds. "You know how crazy dad gets. If he finds out I met someone he's liable to get on the next plane to Hawaii."

Oh, this girl. What am I going to do with her? She has a point, though. Gil tends to overreact just a smidge.

"I won't bring it up, but if he asks—"

"Thanks, mom," she squealed.

"Now spill it. I want to know all about him."

Grace gushed on and on about Makoa and how many things they shared in common.

"I wasn't even supposed to know." I chuckle. "I found out because of a missent text that was meant for Frannie."

"Why the big secret?" He sounds annoyed.

"Relax. It isn't a secret. They'd only just met a few days before."

"And now she's bringing him home?"

"I guess it stuck." I shrug.

"What do you know about him?"

As we weave our way along the roads inside the airport, I tell Gil everything I know. Makoa was born and raised on the big island. He's a marine biologist, and they work together, but she didn't meet him at work. She met him at the beach with some friends.

"I guess she's been feeling homesick. Makoa picked up on it and kept her company all night."

"Hmm." Gil grunts.

"Really?" I roll my eyes.

"Sounds like he found an easy target." I slap his arm. "You don't even know the boy."

"I don't have to. I know what guys his age want."

I'm not going to mention his age. "So, I guess my dad should've been tougher on you?" I chuckle.

"We aren't talking about me. I want to know more about this guy."

"They realized they worked together, but in different areas of the center, which is why they hadn't met before," I explain. "Makoa brought her home. He has a sister Grace's age.

"Grace hasn't been telling us exactly how homesick she's been feeling. So much so that she's reached out to Rutgers to see if her acceptance was still good or if she'd have to reapply.

Even though she lives in what many consider paradise, she only left campus to work. She didn't know anyone and was struggling to fit in on the island.

Going to the beach that night was a fluke. A female co-worker who she'd confided in wouldn't take no for an answer. She didn't want Grace to give up without truly experiencing life on the island. Grace was happy she went. That night changed everything for her. That's when things started to look up.

"Ke'ala, Makoa's sister, and Grace have been spending a lot of time together as well. Actually, his whole family has opened their arms to her."

"She could've just said something to us and come home."

"And given up on a dream? Do you really want that for her?"

Gil finally finds a parking spot. We get out and begin walking to the building.

"I guess not," he says and sighs. "And I'm assuming this guy is staying with her?"

"Yes. She really likes him, so be nice, Gilbert."

"Yeah, yeah, yeah." He grabs my hand. "Let's go get our little girl."

33

Gilbert

G race's flight lands right on schedule. We're standing as close as we can to the gate so I can get a good look at this guy, I mean, so I can see my little girl as soon as she steps off the escalator.

"Daddy," Grace calls and comes running to me.

"Gracie girl." I throw my arms around my daughter and lift her from the ground. "I missed you so much. Let me get a good look at you."

She giggles when I set her down.

"Look at how tan you are," Liz says and wraps her in a hug.

Meanwhile, my eyes have found Mr. Hawaii. I don't know how I missed him. He's well over six feet tall and looks like a solid wall of muscle.

When Grace realizes I'm staring at him, she grabs his hand.

"Dad, I'd like you to meet Makoa.""Nice to meet you." I extend my hand.

"Aloha," he responds and shakes my hand. "It's good to meet you. I've heard a lot about you."

I'm glad he's heard a lot about me since I've just learned of his existence.

Liz steps up. "It's so good to meet you."

He hugs her. "Aloha, Mrs. Benton. It's a pleasure to meet you as well."

"How was your flight?" Lis asks.

"Long," they say in unison.

"Do you have any checked bags?" "Nope. Just these," Grace says and motions to the two backpacks Makoa has slung over his shoulder.

It's a far cry from how Grace typically travels, which usually involves several large suitcases.

When I take a good look at her, I notice the subtleties. Something's different. She's more grown-up. And there's a peacefulness about her I've never seen before. Maybe Hawaii has been good for her?

"Are you two hungry? We can stop somewhere to eat."

She looks to Makoa.

"I could eat." He smiles. "Are you hungry, ku'uipo?"

What did he just call her? I look at Liz, but she just shrugs.

"I can't decide if I'm more hungry or tired."

"Let's go eat. Then we can go home, and you can take a nap," Liz suggests.

"Sounds good," Grace agrees.

We stop at a small café just a few blocks from our house and have a relaxed late lunch.

While we eat, Makoa tells us all about Hawaii and the work he and Grace are doing at the conservation center. Since they met, he was able to have Grace transferred to his department, so now they share a ride to and from work.

"My family loves having Grace stay with us." The words seem to slip out of his mouth.

"Did you say Grace is staying with you?" I ask, trying my best not to lose my cool.

"I am, dad," Grace interrupts. "Living in the dorms was difficult for me. My roommate and I didn't have anything in common, and I was having a hard time fitting in. Not to mention how expensive it was traveling to work. Mr. and Mrs. Haukea have been very generous letting me move in."

Liz puts her hand on my thigh under the table. She's rubbing gentle circles on my leg, I'm sure trying to keep me from losing my temper, but at this moment, nothing she does is going to calm the storm brewing inside me.

"And you didn't think to tell us this little fact?"

"I knew what you would say." Grace waves her hand around. "I didn't want to have to go through this over the phone."

"I see."

Picking up my sandwich, I choose to eat rather than continue this conversation in the middle of the café and make a scene.

Grace and Makoa look between each other. Grace gives a slight shrug. Liz remains quiet.

There's no more conversation while we finish eating. After I pay the bill, we go back outside to the car.

"Makoa and I are going to walk. I want to show him around the neighborhood."

"Take your time," Liz says. "We'll see you two at home."

Grace and Makoa walk away hand in hand while I stand fuming outside the café.

"Let's go to the car," Liz grabs my hand and gives a little tug.

"Did you know this?"

"No, I didn't. It's as much of a surprise to me as it is to you," Liz says as we walk to the parking lot and get in our car. "I can't lie. Knowing she's living with a family instead of on her own in the dorms is comforting."

"Comforting. Right."

The drive home, although short, is wrought with tension. My grip on the steering wheel is so tight I'm surprised it doesn't snap. I'm thankful that I hit every red light because it gives me a few extra minutes to at least attempt to calm down.

Just as I'm finishing parking in front of the house, I see Grace and Makoa rounding the corner.

"Gil, please calm down," Liz implores. "Don't make a big deal out of this."

I turn to face Liz. "Aren't you the least bit upset that she didn't bother to mention this little development? That she just up and moved without telling us?"

Liz is always the one who takes things in stride. I recognize that. But this is a big deal. This is our eighteen-year-old daughter, who's insisted on moving to the other side of the world. To go to school. To live on campus. Now, weeks later, we find out she's not living on said campus, but in the home of this man who's walking down the sidewalk holding her hand.

But I'm supposed to stay calm.

"Did you two have a nice walk?" Liz asks.

"We did. This is a beautiful city," Makoa says. "I can't wait to explore it more while we're here."

"Where are you planning to take him? I know you have limited time?" Liz asks as we walk into the house.

The girls discuss the multiple historical destinations and the museums and which ones they should put as a priority. So far, it sounds like Independence Hall and The Liberty Bell have made the list. They'll visit the Franklin Institute one day, and not surprisingly, they're taking a trip across the George Washington Bridge to Camden to spend a day at the aquarium.

"Sounds like you two have a busy week planned. Will we get to see you at all?"

Liz gives me a warning look.

"We were hoping maybe we could spend the weekend here," Grace says. "Then we'll head over to Stacey's place. She's out of town, so it'll be like we're at an Airbnb."

"Of course, you can stay here." Liz smiles. "Let me go up and put fresh sheets on your bed."

"Thanks, mom." Grace wraps her arms around Liz.

"I can go out and grab our bags if that's okay, Mr. Benton."

"Sure." I hit the button, unlocking the car.

"Thanks. I'll be right back."

As soon as the door closes behind him, Grace turns to us, nearly bouncing.

"What do you guys think? Isn't he wonderful?"

"He seems very sweet, and it's clear he's crazy about you," Liz says. "And he's very handsome."

"What do you think, dad?"

"I guess he's okay."

"Just okay?"

"Just okay." I nod.

Liz heads for the staircase, leaving Grace and me alone.

"Don't you like him, dad?"

"I didn't even know there was a him until the drive to the airport. And then I find out you're living with him. Forgive me if I'm struggling a little right now."

"I'm sorry." Grace sits on the couch. "The night we met, I knew I liked him. I mean, look at him. Who wouldn't?"

I guess if you like tall, dark, well-built, long-haired guys, Makoa fits the bill.

Sitting next to Grace, I ask, "You moved off campus without even telling us. What if you'd have disappeared? Your mom and I would've had no idea where to even start looking."

"That wouldn't have happened. Makoa's family is a well-known and prominent family on the island," she explains. "His dad is a doctor, and his mom is a sought-after artist. I'm perfectly safe with them."

"I don't understand all the secrecy, Grace."

She sighs. "I love you, dad, but you aren't always the easiest to talk to. You aren't good with these kinds of changes. I knew if I told you how homesick I was and then that I was moving in with them, you'd try to talk me out of it."

She's right. I wouldn't have agreed with her leaving campus. Heck, if I knew she was considering coming home and going to Rutgers, I would've bought her a plane ticket.

"I can see what you're thinking," she giggles. "You would've arranged for me to come home and go to Rutgers."

"Guilty." I shrug.

"Give him a chance, please." The door opens. "He's a great guy. I know you'll like him." She jumps up and goes to him. "Come on. I'll show you where our room is."

He follows my daughter upstairs as I process what she's said—our room. I don't know why I thought that maybe he'd sleep in Hunter or Marco's old room. I should've realized they live together in Hawaii, not that she's living in their house, sharing a room with his sister. Nope, she shares a room—a bed with him.

I close my eyes and take a deep breath. Everyone always said things would get easier when the kids got older.

They lied.

It was much easier when they were little and safe under my roof. There was no worry about boyfriends or girlfriends or who was living where. What I'd give to go back in time.

34

Elizabeth

They fought their jet lag as long as they could yesterday. Grace couldn't keep her eyes open any longer when, under great protest, Makoa said they were going to bed. She insisted on spending every possible second with us since her time here is so short.

I'm so thankful Grace and Makoa decided to spend the weekend at home. It's allowing us the opportunity to get to know him better. He's an absolute sweetheart. He's intelligent, well-spoken, and crazy about my daughter.

Tonight, I'm told we're in for a treat. Makoa has offered to cook dinner. The two of them are out buying groceries for a traditional Polynesian meal. I'm an adventurous eater, so I can't wait to see what they're planning.

Meanwhile, Gil and I are fulfilling orders for Real Life Romance. We've been getting so much traffic on the site we're struggling to keep up with the demand. There's so much inventory waiting to be packed that we're running out of room in the office. I think it's time to make some changes in the house.

"What are your thoughts on taking one of the boy's bedrooms and turning it into a storage room for all this merchandise?" I motion to the boxes piled up all over the office.

Gil freezes. "What if they want to move home? Then what'll we do?"

I hold back the laugh that threatens to come out. "Hunter moved to Florida, and Marco's getting married next year. I highly doubt either one will move home, but if by some chance they do, we have other bedrooms." I try to address his concerns. "Right now, it's more important to have room for inventory. Especially since we're adding two more pre-made date boxes."

The first box is an at-home picnic. Included is a set of plastic champagne flutes, a checkered picnic blanket, and a fun couple's game to get the conversation flowing. Those couples who wish, can purchase a spicy add-on that includes a blindfold and a fun toy.

The second box is a couple's spa night. Included are candles, bath salts, bubble bath, and massage oil—everything needed for a sensual bath with your partner. With this box, there's a spicy tier as well. For couples feeling a bit friskier, they can add satin robes, silicone lube, and a waterproof toy.

I'm anticipating a good response to these boxes and am looking ahead to where we will put the inventory while we're filling orders.

Gil hasn't spoken, but I can see the wheels turning in his head. "I guess if we're going to do this, we need to do it right."

That sounds promising.

"The wall between the office and Hunter's room isn't a supporting wall," he says. "It would be easy to open it for an office expansion. This way, we'll have everything in one room." He looks at me expectantly.

I'm stunned. I didn't think he'd suggest something so permanent.

"Really?"

"Sure. Why not?"

This time I can't hold back my laughter. "You never cease to surprise me, Gilbert Benton."

He pulls my wheeled chair closer to him and puts his hands on the armrests, caging me in. "I just want to make you happy."

"You make me incredibly happy." I lean in and kiss him, my hands tangle in his wavy hair that he's letting grow out.

"Gross. Get a room." Grace laughs.

Gil jumps back. "I didn't know you were home."

"That's obvious. Koa and I are going to start cooking."

"What are you guys making?"

"For starters, a salmon and avocado salad. He's going to do his best at replicating Samoan chicken and coconut rice, and since we were able to find Ahi steaks, we'll also have Ahi poke."

"Wow, what's the occasion?" Gil asks.

"There's no occasion," Grace says too quickly. "And I'm making dessert, or at least I'm going to attempt to make one. It's Sefina, Koa's mom's recipe. She had me make it with her several times. I'm pretty sure I can do it on my own."

"It all sounds delicious. I can't wait," I say while Gil eyes Grace suspiciously.

"Well, I better get down there and help him cook."

"Give us a yell when it's ready."

Grace hurries from the office.

"Do you get the feeling those two are up to something?" I ask.

"They better not be. I'm not up for any more surprises."

We've been filling what feels like a never-ending stack of orders for the past few hours, and from the pile of papers still on the desk, it's clear we haven't put a dent in them.

"Mom, Dad," Grace calls. "Dinner'll be ready in five minutes."

"I'll finish this box, and then we'll head down." My stomach chooses that second to growl. "I guess I'm a little hungry."

The closer we get to the kitchen, the more my mouth waters from the rich, fragrant smells wafting through the house.

"I don't know what you two have made," I say as we walk into the kitchen. "But it smells incredible."

"Thank you, ma'am. I hope you like it."

"Makoa's an excellent cook. I'm sure you'll love it," Grace says proudly.

I look on with curiosity as Makoa leans in and touches his nose to Grace's. Together they take a deep breath. He appears to have a very calming effect on our daughter.

Turning to us, Makoa says, "Please sit. I'll serve the meal." Then, he pulls Grace's chair out for her like a true gentleman.

The food is better than anything I've ever tasted. I could quickly get used to eating like this.

"Thank you so much. This was a real treat."

"It's my pleasure," he says and takes Grace's hand in his. "Mr. and Mrs. Benton, there's something I'd like to ask you."

35

Gilbert

There's something I want to ask you? Oh, no. Not this again. It's way too soon.

Without hesitation, he says. "I'd like to ask your permission to marry Grace."

Out of the corner of my eye, I swear I see Lizzie's jaw drop.

I know the feeling very well, sweetheart.

She grabs my arm. I don't know if it's more to comfort me or to keep herself from flipping out.

"Excuse me, did you just ask to marry Grace? You two barely know each other." My voice grows louder with each word. "And how old are you, exactly?"

"I'll be thirty this year."

"You're twelve years older than her." I look at Grace. "What were you thinking?"

"I understand your concern, sir," Makoa says calmly. "But I love your daughter and wish to spend the rest of my life with her."

I turn and look at Liz, whose mouth is still hanging open. She's just staring at the two of them.

"You've been together all of a few months, and you know you want to spend the rest of your life with her?"

"Yes, sir."

"Grace, what do you have to say for yourself?"

"I love him and don't want to wait to marry him."

Okay, something's off here. I lean back in my chair and cross my arms. My eyes dart back and forth, studying my young daughter and this man she's brought home. Someone needs to tell me what's going on. Why they're in such a hurry to get married.

"Grace, can you explain why the rush?" Liz finally speaks.

Grace looks to Makoa. He nods.

"Mr. and Mrs. Benton, Grace and I are going to have a baby."

I spring up so fast my chair nearly falls over.

"What did you just say?" Calm isn't a word in my vocabulary anymore. My voice is raised to a full-on yell.There's no way this stranger just told me he impregnated my daughter.

"Gil, sit down, please." Liz tugs my arm.

"I understand you're upset. My parents weren't exactly proud of me when we first told them either. However." He sits taller. "I will not apologize for creating this new life with Grace. I love her, and I already love the child we made together."

I look at Grace, who's adoringly watching Makoa. A few stray tears drip down her face. When he sees them, he wipes the tears tenderly before he puts his arm around her.

"Can you two excuse me a moment?" I turn to Liz. "Can I have a word with you in private?"

"Excuse us." Liz follows me out of the room.

I don't stop walking until we're outside.

"Can you believe those two in there?" I point in their direction. "He got her pregnant?"

"I'm pretty sure he didn't do that all by himself," Liz says. "Grace had a part in that too."

"And he wants our blessing to marry her? Is he crazy?" I pace back and forth across our tiny front porch. "He's too old. They barely know each other, and they think they want to get married."

"It seems so." Liz leans against the railing. "Gil, can you please stand still? You're making me dizzy."

Stand still? I don't know if I'm physically capable of that right now. My head is spinning. Thoughts are running through it like it's a superspeedway. I can't separate one from another. This may push me over the cliff.

"He's not marrying her, and she's not going back to Hawaii with him. She's moving home." I slice my hand through the air. "And that's final."

Liz pushes off the rail. "That's not going to solve anything, Gil. It'll only push her away." She looks through the front window. My eyes follow hers.

Grace is crying. Makoa has his forehead against hers, his hands on her arms. It's clear he's trying to calm her.

"They're in love," Liz says quietly. "And they're going to be a family. We have no right to get in the way of that."

"They shouldn't have been so careless," I growl.

"That's not fair, Gil," Liz scolds. "Don't you remember how we felt at their age?"

"We were married."

"And they'll be married soon too." She looks at me, determination in her stare. "I will not lose my daughter over this. Yes, this was a big surprise, but Gil." She pauses. "We're going to be grandparents. Our little girl is going to have a baby. Once the initial shock wears off, this'll be something to celebrate."

What? How is this okay at all? I look at Liz like she's a stranger because it feels ,like she is right now. We're so far apart on this one.

"I'm not okay with this, Liz."

She takes a step away from me. "Don't do this, Gil. I'm begging you."

"I won't give them my blessing."

"I'll give them mine. That'll have to do." Liz grabs the handle of the door. "Hopefully, you'll come to your senses before it's too late."

Liz walks into the house, leaving me on the porch, alone. I'm too angry to go back inside, so I go for a walk instead.

36

Elizabeth

I walk back into the house, hoping Gil's behind me, but I don't need to turn around to know he's not there. I don't understand why he's being so unreasonable. I know he has his issues, but refusing to give his blessing? That's something I won't be a part of.

When I walk back into the kitchen, Makoa, and Grace turn to me. Grace's eyes are red and puffy from crying. Makoa holds her protectively against him.

"I apologize for my husband's behavior. You have my blessing to marry Grace."

"What about Dad?"

"I can't speak for him."

"How do we proceed?" Makoa asks, genuinely unsure.

"Let's sit and talk."

I lead them to the sofa. Makoa does his best to explain the traditions of his ancestors. Traditions his family still upholds. One of which is having the blessing of the girl's family before proposing marriage. Not having Gil's blessing presents an issue he isn't sure how to deal with."Can we call my family? I'd like for us to speak with my father."

"I think that's a good idea." I don't want him doing something that would offend his culture or his family.

Makoa pulls out his cell phone and calls home.

"Aloha."

"Aloha, makuakāne. I'm here with Grace and her mother, Mrs. Benton," Makoa explains.

"Aloha, Mrs. Benton," a deep male voice says.

"Aloha. Please call me Liz."

"Then you must call me Liko."

"It's a pleasure to meet you, Liko. You have a wonderful son. I'm enjoying getting to know him."

"I need some advice, makuakāne."

"What is your dilemma, Koa?"

Makoa takes his time explaining the evening's events to his father, who listens quietly on the other end.

"We have Mrs. Benton's blessing, but not Mr. Benton's. I don't know how to proceed." Pain is evident on his face.

"I see," Liko says. "Please hold on. I'm going to go get makuahine."

"He's getting his wife, Sefina," Grace whispers.

"Makoa, kuu keki. We miss you and Grace very much."

"And we miss you as well."

"Your father explained your problem," she says. "I understand his emotions. Your father would feel much the same if this was your sister."

"Sefina, this is Liz. Grace's mom. May I interrupt and explain a little about my husband?"

"Please, share what you can."

Gil's a fairly complicated man to explain, but I do my best to describe his difficulty with change, especially when it's unexpected.

"And with Grace being our youngest, it's a lot for him."

"How will you feel if Makoa and Grace proceed with their engagement and wedding plans?"

"They have my full blessing. I wouldn't worry about Gil. Once he has some time to process it, he'll come around."

"Makuakāne, do you feel it would be proper to proceed?"

"You've done well, Makoa. Given what Liz has said, it will be okay."

"Thank you both," Makoa's smile lights up his face. "I'll call again in a few days."

After they say goodbye, Makoa shocks me when he gets down on one knee in front of Grace.

"Grace, we haven't been together for long, but the heart is not governed by time. You are kuu mea aloha, my beloved, and ko'u mau loa, my forever. Aloha wau iā 'oe, I love you with all I have, with all I am." He takes her hand in his. "Will you marry me?"

Tears stream down Grace's face. "Yes. Yes, I'll marry you."

He slips a ring onto her finger and pulls her into his embrace.

Part of me feels like I'm intruding on this private moment, but I'm also touched to have been included.

When Makoa lets Grace go, she examines her ring.

"Do you like it?" He sounds unsure."It's perfect. I love it." Grace comes over to me. "Look at how pretty it is, mom."

The platinum band looks like a vine with diamonds inlaid throughout. At the center is a heart-shaped diamond. It's unique and completely Grace.

"It's stunning. I'm so happy for you." I wrap my arms around my little girl. "So, when is my grandchild due?"

Grace sits back on the couch and cuddles up next to her fiancé. He wraps his arm around her keeping her close.

"The baby is due in November," Makoa says. "We'd like to be married in August."

"We're planning a beach wedding," Grace adds.

"Isn't that going to be a little close to the next semester starting?"

"I'm not planning on going back to school," Grace says quietly. "I'd like to be home to raise our baby."

Part of me is disappointed that she won't be returning to school, but I understand the desire to be home to raise your child.

"I make enough to support us," Makoa adds. "I'll provide a good life for our family."

His words are comforting.

"As long as this is what you want, Grace. That's all that matters to me."

"It is. After my maternity leave, I'll still work part-time at the conservation center. I love it there and don't want to give that up. Sefina will keep the baby while I'm at work."

Grace has her daddy's honey-colored eyes, and right now, they're sparkling. There's no question this is exactly what she wants.

"I think that plan sounds perfect. What can I do to help?"

"Can we go wedding dress shopping while we're here? I don't want anything too fancy, and it'll have to be able to fit me when I have a bigger stomach." She giggles.

This week has already thrown us some major curveballs. Once the shock wears off, I'm sure Gil will come around. Until then, I'm riding the high of planning to shop for a wedding dress with my daughter and knowing I'll be a Nana in a few months.

37

Gilbert

I sit in my office, staring blankly at my computer screen. My mind won't stop replaying the scene of Grace and Makoa telling me they want to get married and they're having a baby. I should've never agreed to let her go traipsing off to Hawaii. Now, I'm told she's not returning to school. And everyone expects me to be okay with this.

I'm not. I'm not okay with any of it.

To make matters worse, Liz and I aren't on speaking terms. She handled the news our strong-willed daughter sprung on us much better than I did. And she's furious with me for refusing to give my blessing. We've never been so far apart on something. Not only is Liz taking Grace wedding dress shopping, but she's already starting to shop for the baby. I don't know how she can be so happy about this.

Grace had plans. She was supposed to go to college and get her degree. It's what she's worked so hard for. But the first guy that comes along gets her pregnant, and now she wants to marry him. I don't understand it.

"Mr. Benton, your two o'clock is here," Liam says from my open door.

"Can you get them settled in the conference room? I'll be right in."

"Sure thing. Are you okay?"

"What?" I look up. "Yeah, I'm fine."

"Alrighty." Liam closes the door behind him.

This is an important meeting with the mayor and several other city officials regarding Chris's project. Most of them are behind him and his efforts, but we have one or two digging their heels in on some of the proposed designs. Problem is, I'm not in the right headspace for this meeting.

I stop in my private bathroom and splash some cold water on my face. Get it together, Gil. You can't mess this up. After taking a few minutes to slip on the mask of the guy who has it all together, I exit my office and head for the conference room.

After a tense two-hour meeting, we finally adjourn with everyone on the same page. Once I showed the 3D model of Chris's planned neighborhood, complete with community gardens, dog parks, children's playgrounds, and the possibility of a neighborhood charter school, there was no way anyone could deny the benefits this will have for our city. Chris is hopeful that once this project is complete and the city sees its success, it'll pave the way for him to purchase more properties to revitalize. It's an exciting opportunity for Philadelphia, and I'm glad to be a part of it.

When I get back to my office, my daughter is sitting at my desk waiting for me.

"Grace, what are you doing here?"

"I'm only in town for one more day. I don't want to leave with things like this between us."

"I'm disappointed, Grace," I say as I take a seat across from her. "This was not the plan."

Grace leans forward, putting her elbows on my desk. "Daddy, not everything in life has to be planned."

That statement makes my brain want to explode. I'm in firm disagreement with it. Like ours, Grace's life, was planned out—she was part of the planning. School was to be her top priority. She was supposed to earn her degree so she could get a job in the field she loves so much. Men, marriage, and babies were not part of the plan until later. Yet here we are.

"But we had a plan," I stress. "A good one that would set you up for a prosperous future."

Grace sighs loudly. "I know, but plans change. And I'm happy." She stands up and walks around the desk, taking the seat next to me. "Makoa makes me happy. I don't care about a college degree. It's only a piece of paper. I'm still able to do what I love at the center." She pauses. "I didn't plan to meet someone, but I did, and my life is even more full. I'll have a husband and a child."

"How will you support yourselves?"

"Makoa makes good money, enough for us to live a comfortable life."

"How are you going to raise a baby without your family nearby?" Somehow, I have to convince her to stay here, with her family.

"I know you and mom can't move to Hawaii. But I'm hoping you'll visit, as much as possible," she says. "And I do have family there. Makoa's family is also my family. They're giving us their large house and are in the process of building a smaller house on the property for them and his sister."

"Do they plan on helping you with the baby?" I ask.

"Yes. In their culture, Ohana, family, is always a top priority. They'll be a daily presence in our lives. The spirit of Ohana is a beautiful thing to experience."

"Is there any chance I can convince you two to move back here?" I never imagined any of my children living halfway around the world. We won't get to know our grandchild like we should.

"Hawaii is my home now."

Her words cut straight through my heart. She must see that because she grabs my hands.

"Daddy, I'll always love you, and we'll come back to Philly to visit. But Hawaii is our home."

My heart is in shreds. It feels like I'm losing my daughter.

"We're getting married in August. I hope you'll be there to walk me down the aisle."

This is it. The answer I give will make or break our future. Grace watches me with wide amber eyes that are identical to mine.

For a moment, I see a young Grace, pigtails bouncing as she runs into my arms. But the image quickly fades, giving way to the young woman sitting next to me. My daughter's no longer a little girl. She's a grown woman about to become a wife and mother.

"You need to know that I wish you would stay here or at the very least wait on the wedding. This guy is so much older than you, and you barely know him. I think this is a mistake, and I can't give my blessing."

"I didn't think you'd withhold your blessing." She wipes the tears that are sliding down her cheeks.

"I can't give it, Grace. I wish you could understand it from my point of view."

"And I wish you'd look at it from my point of view," she says. "We're a family, and I love him. That won't change. I hope you will, though."

"I'll agree to walk you down the aisle, but that's it."

"That's something, I guess."

Two weeks went by far too quickly, and now I'm watching my daughter walk through the security checkpoint at the airport with her fiancé. The word still doesn't feel right on my tongue.

Liz stands next to me, crying quietly. Goodbyes are never easy for her. We've barely talked since the whole proposal dinner mess. And we're far from being on the same page.

On the way to the airport, I made my feelings perfectly clear to Makoa. I explained that I'll be there to walk Grace down the aisle but that I'm not supporting this marriage. It's too soon, and there's no reason to rush into it. Makoa disagreed, which I expected. I thought my concession would ease the tension between Liz and me, but it didn't. There was an icy chill in the air for the duration of the ride.

The one thing I won't do is lie or hide my feelings. This is my daughter, and if I see her about to make a serious mistake, I won't sit quietly on the sidelines.

We stay until they're out of sight.

"I can't believe you did that," Liz says as she wipes her eyes.

"Did what? Told them how I feel?"

"Yes." She looks at me, her blue eyes dark and angry.

"Don't I get to say how I feel?"

"Oh, you do, and you did, loud and clear." She picks up her pace to put distance between us.

It feels like everyone is pitted against me. Grace brought Makoa to meet both sets of grandparents and tell them about their engagement and that they'll soon be great-grandparents. No one batted an eyelash. No one cared that she's dropping out of school. No one cared that she's marrying a man she's only known for a few months and who's twelve years older than her. The focus was on how handsome Makoa is and what a beautiful bride

Grace is going to make, and what an adorable baby they're going to have.

I sat in the corner and watched while everyone celebrated. Not once did anyone bother to ask my feelings about it. They all assumed I was just as happy as they were. However, nothing could be further from the truth.

"Would you rather I lie to them?"

"Of course not, but how many times do you need to drive your point home?" She stops walking and crosses her arms. "The night he asked for your blessing, you made your feelings known."

"She's making a mistake, Liz."

People around us stop to watch the argument ensuing in the middle of the airport. They whisper as they walk past.

"Gil." She lowers her voice. "Don't you remember when we told everyone we were getting married? All our friends thought we were crazy. It was only our parents who gave us unconditional support."

"What does that have to do with this?"

She lets out a small laugh and shakes her head. "You don't think our parents had doubts or concerns?"

"I don't know."

"Of course they did. We were barely eighteen—we were just kids."

"But we were dating for a few years. We knew each other."

"People date for years, and marriages still fall apart. How long they know each other is doesn't matter. Their ages are irrelevant. They're in love and only want their family's support. Why can't you give them that?"

"I'm walking her down the aisle, isn't that enough?"

"No," Liz says and starts walking away.

I walk behind her, lost in my thoughts.

My parents never expressed any concern about Liz and I getting married. And other than the questions Marco asked on our walk. He never expressed doubts either. That's because things were different, I tell myself. We might have been young, but we'd been dating for a few years. Marriage was the next logical step.

That can't be said for Makoa and Grace. They've only known each other for a few months. There's no possible way they can make this work.

38

Elizabeth

Gil and I have barely spoken two words to each other all week. He's not giving an inch on this. When we got married, we promised each other we'd never go to bed angry, that we'd never allow a disagreement to carry over to the next day. And until this point, we never have. Oh, we've had some fights. Tell me a married couple who hasn't. But we always worked out our problem, even if it meant a sleepless night.

Until now.

I've tried to talk to him, to reason with him, but he won't give an inch. I don't understand why he's digging his heels in so hard on this. It's creating a wedge between him and Grace and an even bigger one between him and me. It's uncomfortable, and I don't like it.

I don't know what to do, so I call my mom.

"Liz, his point of view is understandable," Mom says.

"It's not that I don't have concerns. I'm just choosing to put them aside to give Grace and Makoa my full support."

Marriage is hard enough. They are still getting to know one another, and they have a baby on the way—there are undoubtedly challenging times ahead. They're going to need all the support they can get.

"And that's a wonderful thing to do. But you can't force your husband to feel the same."

"But it's not right, Mom."

"Elizabeth, I love you dearly, but you don't get to decide if what Gil believes is right or wrong."

That's part of what I love about my mom. She's not afraid to tell me when I'm wrong. It's also what I hate because I want someone to tell me I'm right.

"You need to accept Gil's feelings, even if you disagree with him. This has gone on long enough."

After we hang up, I take some time to think about what she said. As usual, she's right. I don't get to play judge and jury. I need to validate my husband's concerns and put this behind us before it goes any further.

I grab the phone to call Gil's office. It rings a few times before someone picks up.

"Mr. Benton's office. Camila speaking. Can I help you?

"The one voice I did not want to hear.

"Hi, Camila. Is Liam there?"

"He's on vacation this week. Is there something I can help you with?"

She's the last person I want to talk to right now, but it seems I have no choice.

"Is Gil there?"

"He's a little tied up right now."

"Do you know what his schedule looks like this afternoon?"

"He should be in his office the rest of the day. Can I give him a message for you?" Her voice is like nails on a chalkboard. It sends shivers down my body.

"No message. I'll stop by and talk to him."

Without so much as a polite goodbye, she hangs up the phone.

I check the time and hurry to take a shower. I'm going to be cutting it close to make it for his lunchtime, so I hurry to dry my hair straight. Then, grab my black wrap dress and a pair of heels. It's time to go make up with my husband.

My ride drops me off in front of Gil's building. I didn't even bother to order food because I don't intend on eating.

When I get up to his floor, the hallways are quiet. Everyone must be out to lunch. The click of my high heels echoes on the tiled hall floor as I make my way down to Gil's office. His door is shut, and I can hear the faint sound of his voice through the door, so I know he's in there.

I turn the knob and push the door open.

With the blink of an eye, my world comes to a screeching halt. My feet go numb, forcing me to hang onto the handle, so I don't fall to the floor.

Gil is sitting in his chair, his hands on her arms. Camila's straddling his legs. Her fingers are entwined in his hair—the hair that my fingers caress. Her shirt hangs open, exposing her red lace bra. Her lips are on his lips—the lips that have only ever been mine.

When I clear my throat, Camila jumps back.

"Oh my god, Liz." She quickly starts buttoning her blouse.

Gil jumps from his seat. "This isn't what it looks like."

For a moment, I'm unable to move. My feet are like lead weights. My brain struggles to process what I've just witnessed. When Gil starts coming toward me, I find the strength to move. I turn and run from the room.

Gil calls after me, but I'm already down the hall and pounding on the elevator button. Please hurry. Please hurry.

The doors open, and I step in just as Gil catches up. He leans on the wall with one hand to catch his breath.

"Liz, wait. Please."

"How could you?"

The elevator doors close.

I didn't have a chance to call for a ride, and I'm not waiting outside Gil's building because I know he'll come looking for me.

I hurry down the street and don't stop until several blocks separate me from Gil's building. Only then do I pull up the app and arrange for a ride. I manage to keep my emotions in check on the drive home, but barely.

Once I'm in the house, I let myself fall apart. The tears won't stop.

My cell keeps ringing, Gil's name flashing across my screen, but I don't answer it. Then the texts start.

(Gil) Liz, please answer the phone.

(Gil) You don't know the whole story. Please let me explain.

(Gil) I'm on my way home. We need to talk.

If he thinks he's coming in here, he's got another thing coming. Anger now rivals the sadness—a rather toxic combination. I hurry up the stairs and into our bedroom, where I grab a duffle from the closet. Opening the drawers, I grab handfuls of Gil's clothes and toss them in the bag. There's no way he's staying here, not after he betrayed me with another woman. Not just any other woman, he ran right into Camila's arms.

When the bag is stuffed full, I go back downstairs and toss it on the front porch before locking the door and putting the chain on to make sure Gil can't get in.

(Liz) Your bag is on the porch.

(Gil) Liz, please. We need to talk.

(Liz) There's nothing to talk about.

(Gil) I need to explain. It wasn't what you thought.

(Liz) Camila was half undressed on your lap. Your lips were on hers. That's all the explanation I need. I made it clear in the beginning that cheating was the one thing I couldn't forgive. We're over.

I power off my phone and toss it on the kitchen counter. Then, I slump onto the floor and give in to the pain that's shredding my heart.

Gil's car pulls up to the house, his tires screech to a stop. He tries the door. It unlocks, but it's no use. The chain is on. He can't get in. The doorbell rings over and over, and he pounds on the door.

"Liz, let me in," he yells. "We need to talk." More pounding. "Please, Liz. Don't do this."

He keeps this up for nearly an hour while I sit sobbing on the floor.

39

Gilbert

She's chained the door shut. "Liz, I know you're in there." I ring the doorbell. "Let me in. We need to talk." I pound my fist while I beg my wife to open the door.

After a half-hour of yelling and hitting my fist on our heavy wood door, the neighbors start coming out of their houses to watch the spectacle occurring on my front porch. I stop before I get the police called on me.

I sit on the steps and drop my head into my hands. What am I going to do? Of all the moments for Liz to walk in, it was right then. What she saw played on her deepest fears. Every time I close my eyes, I see the look of pain on her face. She was utterly destroyed.

I wait on the porch for hours, hoping she'll give in and open the door. After the sun goes down, I realize that's not going to happen. Grabbing my duffle bag, I make my way back to the car. I'm not sure where to go.

When we first got married, my parents told me I was always welcome to come home for anything we needed, but they'd never house me if Liz and I were fighting. They believed we needed to work out our problems together, not avoid them. In our vows, we promised never to go to bed angry with each other. She's never shut me out like this. I don't know what to do.

I consider calling one of the kids, but I don't want to alarm them. The only other place I can go is my office. Looks like I'll be spending the night on my office sofa. Tonight will be a cool-down time, and I can explain everything to her tomorrow.

Liz is my whole life. I refuse to lose her.

The couch in my office is fine to sit on, but it was not made for sleeping. When I get up the following day, my back and neck are killing me. I have about fifteen minutes to change and put myself together before everyone comes in.

When they remodeled the office several years ago, I told them I didn't need a private bathroom, but the powers that be insisted. Today, I'm thankful for it. I do my best to wash up and get dressed for work. I hang my duffle on the back of the door. I'm the only one who uses this room, so there's no chance of someone stumbling upon it and asking questions I don't want to answer.

(Gil) Can you grab me a coffee and bagel on your way in? I'll pay you when you get here.

(Liam) Sure boss. Running late today?

(Gil) I had to come in early to get something done

(Liam) No problem.

I try to call Liz, but she doesn't answer. I text, and they're left unread. Something tells me this isn't going to go away today. Bunking in my office is not something that can happen long-term. I can't call Marco or Frannie, and hotel rooms don't come cheap. My only option is to suck it up and beg my parents to let me stay at their house for a few days—until I can get Liz to listen to me.

"Gilbert, how are you today?" Mom answers the phone. "It's not like you to call so early on a workday."

"I didn't wake you guys up, did I?"

"You know us. We're up with the sun. Is everything ok?"

"Not really." Here goes nothing. "Can I stay with you guys for a couple of days?""That's an odd request."

"Liz and I had a fight."

"I see. Let me get your father. You should speak to him."

I was hoping mom would say yes. She's usually the easier one. Getting dad to say yes will be a bit more challenging.

"Your mom says you asked to come home?" Dad gets straight to the point.

"Yes, sir. Liz and I had a fight. She's refusing to speak to me, and she won't let me come home."

"I see. Are you at fault here, son?"

"Yes, but it was a misunderstanding."

I try to explain what happened with Camila and how Liz walked in on it.

"Are you having an affair?" Dad's voice is stern.

"No. How could you even ask that?" I raise my voice. "I love my wife."

"How did this happen then?"

I do my best to explain Camila, which is difficult because I don't understand it all myself. I try to repeat everything Liz has said to me about her, hoping it makes sense. Just as I'm finishing, there's a knock on my office door.

"Hang on a second, dad." I put the call on mute and unlock my door to answer it.

"Breakfast." Liam holds out my coffee and a brown bag that contains the food. "You look rough. Are you ok?"

"I didn't sleep well last night, and I had to come in early. Made for a rough morning." It's not a lie. "Thanks, I'll send you the money."

"It's on me."

Liam heads to his desk, and I close the door to get back to my call.

"Sorry about that."

"I spoke to your mom. You can stay here for a few nights, but your priority is to fix this with your wife."

"I'm trying, dad."

"We'll see you after work, son."

My day is packed with meeting after meeting. I find myself struggling to stay focused on work. All I want to do is fix this with Liz, not listen to people giving presentations about housing. The only good thing about today is Camila called off.

Speaking of Camila, yesterday she crossed a line, but I don't know the proper way to handle this. I'll have to call, Tessa, my supervisor, to discuss what's going on and what disciplinary action we can take.

In between meetings, I continue trying to contact Liz, but she's still refusing to take my calls. Although it's cliché, I order a bouquet of flowers with a note begging her to talk to me. Something has to break through the wall she's put up.

Finally, work is over for the day, something that usually brings relief because I know I'm going home to my wife. Today, there's no relief as I drive to my parents' house. It doesn't feel right.

I'm left unsettled.

40

Elizabeth

"I can't forgive cheating, Kelly." I swipe at the tears that keep falling.

"I still don't believe it. Gil never seemed like that guy."

"How am I supposed to tell the kids?" I run my hands through my tangled hair.

I've been in the same clothes for days. I haven't showered or brushed my hair. I don't have the energy or desire to do anything.

"I can come over and be your support while you tell them."

"Thanks, but it's something I have to do myself."

After we hang up, I lay back on the bed and close my eyes. How do I tell my kids their father is having an affair, and we're getting a divorce? Maybe I should leave out the affair part? I don't want to damage their relationship with him just because he and I are breaking up.

"Gil, why did you do this to us?" I ask aloud to the empty room.

I never imagined this happening. This certainly was not in the all-important plan. That's when my anger wins the battle over grief. Gilbert is the one who planned each step of our lives out from the day we got married. Every move we made from when to get pregnant, how many children, how they'd be educated—every single thing was planned out at his insistence. I knew his issues and went along with them.

For what?

Just last week, he had the audacity to lay into Grace for changing plans. Refused to give his blessing for her to get married. Is still refusing to give his blessing because her getting married now wasn't the way he had planned.

But then he gets to go and do this. Well, this isn't in my plan.

Our marriage is supposed to last until death do us part. We're supposed to be together. Until Mr. I Don't Like Change decides to change everything. He has no right.

I'm in the middle of letting myself be mad when my doorbell rings. I check the app to see who's there. It's a delivery person holding a large bouquet.

"Can you leave those on the porch, please?" I use the voice feature to give my instructions.

"Yes, ma'am." The young man carefully sets the vase on the small table on my porch.

After I'm sure he's gone, I drag myself out of bed and down the stairs. It takes a minute to undo the chain and unlock the door before poking my head around the door to make sure there's no one there. Then I step outside. I don't have to look at the card to know who they're from. He sent my favorite, yellow roses.

My friends have always been jealous because Gil is the man who sends flowers for no reason other than to say he loves me. And any other time, I would love the sentiment, but not today.

Carrying the vase into the house, I lock and chain the door behind me. I don't want any surprise guests. My curiosity wins, and I open the envelope that holds the small card. Pulling it out, I read it.

Liz, I need the chance to talk to you. To explain what you walked in on. I love you. I always will. ~Gil

It wasn't what I thought? I was there. I saw with my own two eyes what it was. I don't need him to refresh my memory or to try to explain his way out of it. I crumple the card and toss it in the garbage. I almost toss the flowers, but they're too pretty to waste. An idea comes to mind.

For the first time in days, I take a desperately needed shower and put on some clean clothes. After I dry my hair, I grab the flowers and take a walk down the street.

Mrs. Sheldon, a sweet widow, lives a few doors down. She's lived here forever, long before we bought our house. Over the years, we've gotten to know her. She never had children of her own and became a third grandmother to my kids.

I climb the few steps to her front porch and knock. It takes several minutes before I see her coming toward the door.

"Elizabeth," she says as she pulls the door open. "What a wonderful surprise. Please come in."

"I just came to give you these." I hold out the vase of flowers.

"They're lovely. Would you mind carrying them in for me?"

"Sure." I didn't want to go in, but since Mrs. Sheldon uses a walker these days, she needs assistance with the vase.

I set it in the center of her kitchen table. The bouquet immediately cheers up the tiny space.

"Don't they look beautiful," she says. "Please sit. Have some tea with me."

"I need to get back home."

"Surely you can take a few minutes." Mrs. Sheldon doesn't wait for an answer. Leaving her walker by the table, she shuffles to the sink to put water in the teapot, then puts it on the stove to heat up.

We've had tea many times before, so I help her gather the cups, sugar, and spoons while she gets the teabags. When the pot whistles, I use the hot pad and bring it to the table, pouring us each a cup.

She sits across from me, dunking her tea bag up and down in her China cup.

"I don't want to overstep, dear, but I heard Gil yelling the other night. That boy never raises his voice. Is everything okay?"

This is exactly why I didn't want to come in. I knew the questions would come, and I'm not ready to answer them. I look into Mrs. Sheldon's dark eyes and see nothing but compassion.

"Not really." I take a deep breath, trying not to cry again.

"You and he are so much like my Reginald and I. God rest his soul." She closes her eyes for a brief moment. "It's not like you and Gilbert to fight."

She's right. Thinking back through our twenty-seven years of marriage, we've had our share of small disagreements. That's normal, but I can count on one hand the big fights we've had. We rarely raise our voices at one another. Have never slept apart. Don't go to bed angry.

The anger I feel morphs into grief—the pain stabs my heart. Mrs. Sheldon puts her hand over mine. Despite the wrinkles from age, her skin is as soft as a baby's.

"I'm a good listener," she encourages me.

"Gil did something," I say quietly. "Something I can't forgive."

"I see." She takes the teabag out of her cup and sets it on the saucer. "Marriage is not always a smooth road. There are often bumps along the way."

"This is more than a bump, Mrs. Sheldon." I take a sip of my tea. "I walked in on Gil with another woman."

Mrs. Sheldon gasps. "I don't believe it."

"I wouldn't have either if I didn't see it myself."

I retell the story of how I walked into his office and saw him with Camila. By the end, I'm an emotional mess again.

"Are you certain it was what you thought? Women like that can be savvy. Have you talked to him? Listened to his side of the story?"

"No. I don't want to talk to him."

"Elizabeth, you and Gilbert have spent a lifetime together. There may be a very reasonable explanation for what you saw." Her tone leaves no room for argument. "Life is too short."

"I can forgive almost anything but not infidelity."

"Give him the chance to explain before you make any permanent decisions."

We finish our tea, and I give her my assurance to consider her advice.

When I get back to the house, my cell phone is ringing. I assume it's going to be Gil, but when I pick it up, I see it's Marco.

I swipe the screen to answer the call.

"Hello?"

"Hey, mom. How are you?"

"I'm okay."

"I've been calling you for the past half hour. I was starting to get worried."

"I walked down to visit Mrs. Sheldon and left my cell at the house."

"I called Dad, but he said to call you."

"Did you need something?"

"I was going to let you guys know I'm coming over, but when you didn't answer, I started driving. I'm here now. See you in a minute."

He disconnects before I can say anything. This can't be happening. Marco has always been like a little lie detector. He's going to ask where his father is and why I'm not with him. We never go anywhere without each other.

He tries the front door and finds it locked. Then he rings the doorbell.

After a deep breath and hopefully putting on a mask, he won't see through. I undo the locks and open the door.

"Are you afraid of the boogeyman or something?""What do you mean?"

"You never keep the door chained up."

"There was an attempted robbery in the neighborhood. Can never be too safe," I say as I turn to walk into the living room.

"Where's dad?" Marco asks as he follows me and plops down on the couch.

"He went to see your grandparents."

"Without you?""I wasn't feeling well, so I stayed home."

"You weren't feeling well, but you went to see Mrs. Sheldon?" he asks and raises his eyebrow.

I'm a terrible liar. One question, and I've already messed up my story.

"What's going on, Mom?"

"Your dad and I had a little disagreement. He went out for a bit to calm down."

"I see." Marco sits back and crosses his arms. "He's been out for longer than a bit."

"What are you talking about?" I'm trying to play dumb, but Marco isn't buying it at all.

"Grams called. She's worried about you two. Said dad's been there all week."

Why in the world would my mother-in-law drag our kids into this? I was hoping to keep it from them as long as possible.

"What's going on? The truth, please."

The truth. I don't want to tell him the truth. He's close to his father, and I fear the truth might damage their relationship—no matter what happens between Gil and me, I don't want his relationships with his kids to falter. It's bad enough he and Grace are still on thin ice over the wedding.

The wedding, that's the perfect excuse.

"I'm sure Grace told you how he acted about her getting married."

"She did, but she said he agreed to walk her down the aisle. She's not worried. She knows he'll come around eventually."

"He and I have been arguing about how he handled the whole situation."

"And this disagreement is so bad that he's staying at Gram and Pop's?"

I nod. If I keep talking, it's only going to make it worse.

"For some reason, I don't buy it. Gram didn't tell me what, but she made it seem like something much more."

"I don't know." I shrug. "Was there something you needed that you were coming over today?" I do my best to change the subject.

"I was offered a sort of job transfer," Marco says. "Ivy and I are going to be moving."

Marco is a corporate consultant. Getting transferred is always a possibility, so this news doesn't come as a huge surprise.

"That's exciting. Where are they putting you?"

"Japan."

"Did you just say Japan?"

"Yes. I was offered an incredibly exciting opportunity to teach English in a Japanese elementary school," he says. "Ivy and I want to travel, so this works out perfectly."

"You're not a teacher, though." I'm confused.

He explains the organization that hired him doesn't require a teaching degree for their programs.

"I've been looking for a change, so when I saw the job offering, I applied."

"Wow, I don't know what to say."

"We're super happy. We've always wanted to travel. The company pays for some of our moving expenses and gives us a monthly housing stipend."

"I see why you couldn't pass it up. What is Ivy going to do for work?"

"We're not sure yet. We have enough in savings that even if she doesn't find a job right away, we'll be fine."

For once, one of our kids has managed to surprise me. "When do you two leave?"

"The next term starts in September, so we're planning on leaving the last week of July. That'll give us some time to find an apartment and get acclimated to the culture before school starts."

"Will you be able to make it to Grace's wedding?"

"That's the only bad part. I don't think we'll make it to the wedding."

"Grace is going to be so disappointed."

"I've already talked to her. If she wasn't okay with it, I wasn't going to take the job," he explains. "She was a little upset but said she'll have Liam connect us with a video call."

"That's perfect."

Having our kids so close in age worked out well. It was difficult when they were little. Four toddlers can quickly overtake one parent. And there were some days their mutinies won. But it was all worth it to see how close they are today.

They'll always be siblings, but once they started moving out, they chose to keep in touch—to be friends.

"I'm going to miss you and Ivy, but I'm excited for your new adventure."

41

Gilbert

Marco called to see if Liz and I were home. He wanted to stop by. I've learned when one of the kids wants to 'stop by," it means they have a bomb to drop. Unfortunately, Marco wouldn't tell me anything, and Liz won't answer my calls, so I have no idea what's going on.

I thought about driving over but figured I'd be met with a locked door, and if Marco is there, I don't want to cause a scene in front of him. I'd rather the kids not get dragged into this—whatever this is between us right now.

"Gilbert," My father calls from downstairs.

"Be right there." Living under my parents' roof makes me feel like a teenager again, and I'm not enjoying it. I want to be home with my wife where I belong.

When I get downstairs, I find dad sitting in his recliner.

"Did you need something?"

"Have you talked to your wife yet?"

"I've tried, but she won't take my calls."

"Here's your keys." He holds his hand out. "You've been here a week. The longer you let this go on, the worse it's going to get."

"I can't force her to talk to me."

"Go, son."

My dad dangles the keys in front of me, and I swipe them from his hand, earning a reprimand.

"And get your attitude back in check before you do."

"Sorry."

I leave the house and get in my car, but I have no intention of going to the house. Liz isn't going to let me in. and I don't feel like creating another spectacle. I drive around for a few hours before my cell rings. Pulling into the nearest parking lot, I answer it.

"Hello?"

"Hey, dad."

"How are you, Marco?"

"I'm really confused."

He must have been to see his mom. I don't know what she's told him, but I'm sure that I'm about to find out.

"What are you confused about?"

"Mom said you're staying at Gram and Pop's because you're fighting about Grace getting married."

She didn't tell him what happened with Camila?

"That's what started it."

"I know there's more to the story, but mom refused to talk. Will you tell me what's going on?"

I spend the next half hour telling Marco about Camila and Liz's issues with her. Then, I explain to him what she walked in on.

"The woman was on your lap, half undressed. I understand why she's mad."

"But nothing is going on between us." Why can't anyone seem to understand this?

"You were kissing her?"

"It wasn't like that. You know I'd never cheat on your mom."

"I never thought you would, but I have to be honest, dad, something isn't adding up." He pauses. "I have to go. I need some time to process this."

Marco doesn't even say goodbye before he hands up. How can my family even entertain the idea of me cheating on Liz?

Pulling out of the parking lot, I resume driving through the city. Eventually, I find myself pulling up in front of my house. It's getting dark, and there are lights on downstairs.

Liz is in there, just steps from where I sit in the car. A war rages in my head. Should I get out of the car and demand she opens the door to hear my side of the story, or do I respect the boundaries she put up?

I've never been much for confrontation, so I find myself sulking in the driver's seat of my car, watching my house. Hoping for any glimpse, I can get of my wife. We've never been apart for this long. My heart aches from not talking to her or touching her.

42

Gilbert

Eight weeks. That's how long it's been since Liz kicked me out of the house. I couldn't keep staying at mom and dad's. I'm sure they didn't mean to, but they slipped back into parent mode. We have a good relationship, and I want to keep it that way, so I started looking for somewhere else to stay.

Fortunately for me, Chris has an extra bedroom and is currently single. So, for the time being, I'm staying at his place.

I call Liz every day, hoping that she'll answer, but I get her voicemail each time. Every day after work, I drive by and sit outside the house, willing her to come outside, but it doesn't happen. I don't know if she sees me there or not. It gives me a little solace knowing I'm at least close to her.

The next day when I call, I get the message that her voicemail box is full. She isn't even listening to my messages. I've called the florist shop so much they know me by name. Every other day Liz gets a flower delivery, but my kids tell me that she gives them all to Mrs. Sheldon, the little old lady up the street. It's a kind gesture, but the flowers are for Liz, not Mrs. Sheldon. I also send her a daily email with a read request receipt, which I never get. I don't know if she's reading or deleting them, but I have to keep trying to get through to her.

I need to talk to her.

I need to explain what she saw and what she didn't see—that's something that can't be done over voicemail or through email.

It needs to be face-to-face, but I'm running out of ideas. I'm beginning to wonder if she'll ever speak to me again.

Chris lives on the opposite side of town, so the commute is a bit longer. I hit construction on the way over this morning, so I end up almost twenty minutes late for work.

I hurry out of the elevator and rush to my office. There's a meeting scheduled in a half-hour I need to prepare for, and I don't like to be late.

"Mr. Benton," Liam says as I'm passing his desk. "I have something for you."

"What is it?" I snap at him.

I'm in a sour mood and know I need to reign it in.

He hands me a slip of paper. "Ms. Langley scheduled a meeting with you at two o'clock."

"Thanks, Liam." I take the paper. I've been waiting for this meeting for weeks. "Call me when the zoning officials get here."

"Will do."

I get settled in my office when there's a knock on my door.

"Come in," I call.

The door opens, and Camila strides in carrying a file.

"I have everything ready for the meeting this morning."

"Thank you," I say curtly. "Please wait in the conference room. I'll be there shortly."

But instead of leaving, she comes closer. It's almost like a replay of that fateful afternoon.

"We were interrupted the other day," she says and licks her lips. "I was hoping maybe we could pick up where we left off."

"Camila, go to the conference room." My tone is clipped.

"Whatever you say." She spins on her heel and sways her hips in the too-short dress she's wearing.

I can't wait to meet with Tessa Langley this afternoon. I called her after the incident with Camila, and it's taken this long to get a meeting with her. I know she has channels she needs to go through. Tessa asked me not to confront Camila and to assign her to someone else in the department until we met. Hopefully, she has a resolution for this situation.

At one forty-five, I can't wait any longer. I take the elevator up the three floors to Tessa's office. Her door is open, but I still knock.

"Come on in, Gil," she says. "Please close the door."

"How are you this afternoon?" I ask as I sit down in one of the plush chairs across from her desk.

"I'm well." She sits up straight. "I've had a chance to review your formal complaint."

"Okay."

"What I didn't mention when we first spoke is that I've received several other complaints from people in your department regarding Ms. Steven's inappropriate behavior."

I was unaware of this. "Why didn't they come to me?"

"Because the complaints all involved her behavior toward you. They felt it would be more appropriate to come to me."

"I see." I'm honestly shocked.

I guess I'm the only one who was blindsided by what happened.

"Most of the complaints cited comments that were overheard in passing or observations. None of it was concrete enough to act on. My hands were tied until you called," she says. "We have two ways we can handle this situation. Camila's sexual advance is grounds for her to be terminated."

I don't think Camila is an inherently bad human being. She's young, and she's made poor choices. If she's fired from this job for sexual harassment reasons, she'll never be able to find a decent job again. Some people might think she deserves that, but I don't want this to ruin her life.

"What's option two?""Option two is we call her into my office and have a chat about workplace behavior. Then, we give her the choices. She'll either be terminated, effective immediately, or she'll be sent to take a special training class about sexual harassment in the workplace. After she completes it, she'll be transferred to another office across town."

"Let's do option two."

Tessa nods and then picks up her phone. "Liam, please send Ms. Stevens up to my office."

She then makes another phone call. "Charlene, I'm ready for you."

Charlene runs the ADA compliance department. Her requested presence tells me Camila will be offered a transfer there.

The door opens, and Charlene walks in. I stand to shake her hand.

"It's nice to see you, Char. How's the baby?"

"He's turning one next week."

"Already?" I could've sworn she just returned from maternity leave.

"It goes by fast."

"You're right. It sure does. Before you know it, he'll be going off to college."

She laughs. "Let's get him sleeping through the night first.

Another knock on the door interrupts us.

"Come in," Tessa calls."

When the door opens, Camila's standing there, a smile on her face. When she looks between the three of us, the smile disappears, replaced with a mask of indifference.

"Please come in and have a seat, Ms. Stevens," Tessa says.

I've never seen Camila thrown off her game. She takes tentative steps to the only empty chair in the room, which is on the other side of Charlene.

"I'm sure you're wondering what this is all about?"

"Yes, Ms. Langley, I am."

Tessa recounts the anonymous complaints against her before addressing the situation that occurred in my office.

Camila's stoic the entire time Tessa speaks.

"What you did is grounds for termination, do you understand that?"

"Yes," Camila says flatly.

"I'm prepared to offer you an alternative."

Tessa explains the job offer. Then, Charlene jumps in.

"Should you choose to accept this, you must understand this is a provisional offer."

"How so?" Camila asks with a bit of an attitude.

Both Charlene and Tessa have been employed by the city of Philadelphia for many years. They've worked their way to prestigious positions in a world that was previously male-dominated. They've earned the respect of everyone who operates under their leadership. Camila's attitude isn't going to fly with either of these women.

"Because of the complaints against you, you'll be on one year of probation," Charlene explains. "Every thirty days, you'll meet one-on-one for a progress evaluation."

"I feel that's a bit harsh. These complaints," she says with venom and looks directly at me. "Are they related to job performance?"

"If you'd like, we can go over your six-month review. There are several areas where you scored deficiently," Tessa says and raises her eyebrows.

"That won't be necessary."

"The choice is up to you, Ms. Stevens," Tessa adds.

"Fine. I'll take the transfer."

Tessa slides some papers across her desk and motions to the pens in the house-shaped holder. "I'll need you to read through the job offer, and if you agree, sign on the last page."

Camila scans each page before scribbling her name on the signature line. Then she pushes the contract back to Tessa, who leans forward.

"Ms. Stevens, as a woman, I'm appalled by your behavior. What you did to Mr. Benton and his wife I find unforgivable, and if it was solely up to me, you would no longer be employed." She motions to me. "Fortunately, Mr. Benton is much more forgiving and asked me to find an alternative to firing you. Don't mistake his kindness as any form of attraction to you. Now, listen closely, Ms. Stevens. If there's so much as one complaint regarding improper behavior, you will be fired immediately. Do I make myself clear?"

"Crystal," Camila answers.

This girl is pushing her luck.

"Ms. Stevens," Charlene adds. "I have strict standards for my department. The first of which is we work as a team. All attitudes and anything that detract from that team mentality are left at the door. Take the weekend to get adjusted to that idea." She pulls out her cell and swipes across the screen, typing something. "I've just sent my office's dress code to your work email. I suggest you read it through before coming in on Monday."

"I will," Camila says quietly.

If she allows it, working with these women will teach her some lessons that will guide her in life, far outside the office walls. I genuinely hope she embraces this opportunity.

"That'll be everything. Go home and prepare for your new start on Monday," Tessa says.

"What about my personal things?" Camila asks.

"Your desk will be packed, and your personal belongings will be sent to the new office."

Camila stands and walks toward the door. Before opening it, she turns to me. "I hope we can still be friends, Gilbert."

"I wish you nothing but the best in the future," I say. "But as far as us having any further communication, that's a no. I love my wife and what you did was inexcusable—you crossed a line.

Camila nods and walks out of the office.

"That woman is something else," Tessa says and shakes her head. "I wasn't joking when I said I would've fired her. I give her a month in your office Char." Tessa laughs.

"She's either going to get it together very quickly, or she'll be searching the classifieds for a new career." Charlene shakes her head. "My money is on the latter. Gil, while you're here, can we discuss some specifics on Chris's project. There are a few minor issues with ADA compliance we need to take care of."

Charlene gives me some notes on areas that need attention. By the time we're done, it's time to go home. Well, back to Chris's house.

43

Elizabeth

"Are you sure you want to do this?" Kelly asks as we stand outside the attorney's office.

"Yes. No. But it's what I have to do."

"Talk to him, Liz. Give him a chance to tell his side of the story."

"For what? For him to tell me the kiss meant nothing, and it won't happen again? I ask, frustrated.

"Yes." Kelly grasps onto both my arms. "You and Gil have been together since we were kids. Don't you think it's unfair to file for divorce without even talking to him?"

The tears I've been holding back start to fall. I've been an emotional train wreck since that day. I can't sleep because all I see in my dreams is Gil and Camila together.

He's been relentless in his attempts to contact me. I've gotten so many flowers I could probably open my own florist shop.

Mrs. Sheldon has received a new flower arrangement every other day for weeks. When I brought yesterday's delivery, I heard her mumbling that people were going to start thinking she was opening a funeral home if I kept this up. I guess I need to figure out something else to do with them.

My inbox has several hundred emails from Gil. He's even resorted to sending me old-fashioned handwritten letters.

We've never gone this long without talking to each other, and a part of me desperately longs to hear his voice. To have him tell me I didn't see him and Camila. That it was a bad dream. But I know better. I know what I saw, and there's no explaining his way out of it.

Her shirt was open. His lips were on hers. That's as clear as it gets.

Even still, my stomach is in knots, and my hands are trembling as I turn away from Kelly and open the door to the attorney's office.

My head is on information overload listening to the lawyer spit out facts and figures. Do I want to sue for alimony? Does Gilbert have retirement accounts? Because if he does, I'm entitled to a portion of them. On and on, he keeps going until I interrupt him.

"I don't want any of his money. He worked hard for it. It should go to him," I explain.

"Mrs. Benton, you're going to need a way to support yourself without your husband's income."

"I make enough income from a website I run."

"That's admirable, but—"

"There are no buts," I interrupt him. "I don't want any of Gil's money. I'll put the house on the market, we'll split whatever's left after the mortgage is paid off, but that's it. I'm not out to ruin him."

The attorney leans forward, putting his elbows on his desk. "I may be out of line, but I have to ask. Are you sure you want to divorce your husband?"

"No, she isn't," Kelly chimes in.

"Yes, I'm sure." I look between the two of them. "I caught him with another woman. That's not something I can get past."

"You assume you caught him with another woman."

"I know what I saw, Kelly," I snap. "Can we please get the paperwork ready?"

The attorney slides the stack of papers across his desk. He explains each page as I go through them.

"Do you have a pen?" I interrupt him.

He hesitates before handing me one.

I don't want to hear all the legalese and skip right to the last page where I sign my name on the line and then pass the document back.

"What happens now?"

He explains that the petition will be filed with the courts and Gil will be served. After he signs, there's a ninety-day waiting period before the divorce is finalized.

Kelly and I stand to leave.

"I'll call you when I hear something," he says.

I nod, unable to speak for fear of crying. This is the single hardest thing I've ever done.

When we get in Kelly's car, the dam breaks. I cry so hard I can't catch my breath.

"Liz, please rethink this," Kelly pleads with me. "In your heart, you know this isn't right."

I can't answer her. My heart and head are in conflict with each other, and I don't know if I'll ever be able to resolve it.

44

Gilbert

"Why don't we go out tonight?" Chris asks.

It's Friday night. Chris usually goes out to a bar or a club. He may be in his 40s, but he's not ready to settle down yet.

"You can go. I'm going to stay in."

"I'm not leaving you home alone to sulk. We don't have to stay out late." Chris persists. "We'll get a bite to eat and have a few beers, then come home. You can be my wingman."

"Fine." As much as I don't want to go out, it's the least I can do to repay Chris for letting me stay here.

Chris pulls up the ridesharing app. "They'll be a car here in ten minutes."

"Okay."

"Aren't you going to get changed or anything?"

"What's wrong with my clothes?"

"Jeans and a T-shirt aren't going to attract a woman." He laughs.

"I'm not looking to attract anyone. I'm married." And I plan on staying married.

"Married but very much separated. There's nothing wrong with having a little bit of fun." Chris waggles his eyebrows.

"If that's why you think I'm going out, you're wrong." I'm ready to call this whole night off. I'd be much happier staying in and ordering a pizza.

Chris raises his hands in surrender. "Fine."

We make our way outside, where our ride is waiting for us.

It's no surprise when we're dropped off on South Street. There's no shortage of bars and restaurants here. With the warm weather, many restaurants have outside seating making the street feel like one big party.

Chris picks the Pink Flamingo. It's crawling with people. I can already tell this was not a good idea. Clubs and bars were never my scene.

While all my friends were out partying, I was happy at home with my wife and kids—which is where I want to be right now. Instead, I'm here.

We grab two seats at the bar, and Chris orders us each a beer.

"Dad, what are you doing here?"

I turn around to see Marco and Liam standing behind us.

"What are you two doing here?"

"Marco and I are having a going away party," Liam says, his words a bit slurred.

Liam and Marco met in college. They were both studying business. At the time, Liam had not come out and was struggling. You'd think young adults would be more accepting and supportive, but they gave him such a hard time he ended up dropping out. He and Marco stayed close, which is how Liam came to work in my office. He's a good kid and a good friend to Marco.

"What are you doing at a club?" Marco yells over the band that's now playing.

I motion next to me. "Chris dragged me out."

Chris is already chatting it up with a blonde who's gotta be only half his age. She's wearing a skirt so short it barely covers parts that should be covered, and her shirt is so tight her cleavage is spilling out. Chris doesn't seem to mind. On the contrary, his eyes haven't reached her face yet.

"This is how you plan on getting mom back?" Marco asks.

"There's no harm in me coming out and having a drink," I lie. He and I both know if Liz finds out I'm here, it'll only make things worse.

Marco shakes his head in annoyance. He and Liam walk away.

I can't do this anymore.

"Chris." I tap his shoulder. "I'm gonna head back to the apartment."

"Already? Jenny here has a friend—"

"No."

"Fine. Don't wait up for me."

I nod and walk away in search of Marco and Liam. They're sitting at a table in the back corner.

I'm heading out, I just wanted to say goodbye."

Marco told me what happened," Liam says.

He did?" I look at my son, wondering what exactly he told Liam.

I told him both sides of the story," Marco adds.

And?" I look to Liam.

I "explained to Marco exactly what Camila is and that I'm certain nothing is going on between the two of you." He takes a swig from his bottle. "But man, is that woman gutsy."

Yeah, she's made a mess of everything."

You need to tell mom."

If she'd talk to me, I could."

Tell her on a voicemail or in an email. However you can get the message to her."

No. It has to be face-to-face."

Marco rolls his eyes. "Your stubbornness isn't helping."

Goodnight, boys." I turn and begin to make my way out of the bar.

Women are everyone. Several try to get my attention, grab my arm, or rub up against me as I cross the dance floor, but I shrug them away. There's only one woman I want, and she's not here.

I'm thankful when I finally open the club's door and am hit with a refreshing gust of the cool evening air.

Knowing there's no real food at Chris's apartment, I decide to grab a bite to eat before I call for a ride. I walk down South Street until I find a quiet little diner on the corner. This is more my speed. I'm seated quickly—a table for one.

One is truly a lonely number.

45

Gilbert

anging on the apartment door wakes me up. That's when I realize I fell asleep on the couch. I was watching a movie waiting for Chris, who never came home. I unlock the door and laugh as I pull it open.

Forget your—" I start to ask, assuming it's Chris and that he's lost his house keys but I'm surprised to see a young man in a courier uniform.

I'm looking for Mr. Gilbert Benton," the man says.

That's me."

He hands me a manilla envelope.

What's this?"

They don't pay me to know what it is." He turns and walks down the hallway as I quickly open the envelope.

My eyes scan the document. Liz filed for a divorce.

Hey," I yell. "I don't want these. I'm not signing them."

Call your lawyer," he calls over his shoulder as he steps into the elevator.

I don't have a lawyer.

I don't want a lawyer.

I'm not getting a divorce.

Slamming the door, I go to the couch where I left my cell phone and dial Liz's number. It rings and rings until her voicemail answers. This time there's room to leave a message, and I do.

Liz, I was just given divorce papers. I'm not signing these." I throw them onto the coffee table. "Please call me. We need to talk about this. You have to stop shutting me out. Please, Lizzie."

Beep.

I've used my allotted time. I sink back on the couch and drop my head into my hands. Tears prick my eyes as a feeling of hopelessness settles inside. This cannot be happening.

I've loved Liz from the first day I saw her and Kelly in the hallway at school. She was wearing jeans and a pink top with short ruffle sleeves. Her silky black hair hung in loose curls. Then, she looked at me with her sapphire blue eyes. I didn't even know her name, but even at sixteen years old, my heart knew it had found its mate.

We've been together ever since.

Until now.

Since we got married, we've never spent a night away from each other. Never let arguments carry over until the next morning. What's happening right now is not us, and I don't know how to stop it.

46

Elizabeth

I'm sitting at lunch with Francesca, Ryker, Marco, and Ivy. They're leaving tomorrow to start their new lives in Japan.

"Can you speak any Japanese, Marco?" Frannie asks her brother.

"Ivy and I have been taking some lessons online. We're not experts, but we can ask for basic things."

"I'm sure we'll do better once we're immersed in the culture," Ivy adds.

"Are you nervous?" Ryker asks. "I'd be terrified to move so far away. Especially to a place I've never been."

"Nah. We're looking forward to the adventure." Marco grabs Ivy's hand. "As long as we're together, that's all that matters."

My heart aches. A piece of me is missing. Gil is missing.

I got a text earlier today that the divorce papers were delivered to him. I'm hoping he signs them right away. We're all going to be in Hawaii together in two weeks for the wedding, and I don't want this hanging over us. The divorce won't be final, but at least the papers will be signed.

"Mom." Marco waves his hand in front of my face.

"I'm sorry. I spaced out a minute there."

"I asked if you talked to Dad yet."

Everyone's eyes bore into me waiting on my answer.

"No. I told you I don't want to talk to him."

"That's not how either of you ever taught us to solve a problem," Frannie adds. "Remember when Grace and I would fight, they'd send us to our room and not let us out until we made up."

The kids all share a laugh.

"It's not as simple as that, Francesca. There's nothing he can say that'll fix this." I swallow over the lump in my throat. "I won't stay with someone who's cheated on me."

Marco and Frannie exchange a look. I know they don't agree with my refusing to talk to Gil, and for that matter, they don't agree with Gil for not talking to me. I understand we're their parents, and they don't want to see us split up.

Neither do I.

Never did I imagine this is what my life would look like. Gil is, was, my forever. I fell head over heels for that red-haired amber-eyed boy. Each day we were together, I fell in love with him a little more. We've been together for more than half our lives. His absence hurts. It feels as if a part of me died the day I walked into his office.

That horrible mix of sadness and anger comes back, and I have to force myself to push it back down. I don't want the kids to see it. Even though Gil and I are over, he'll always be their father. I won't do anything to get in between that.

Lunch is over too soon. Before I know it, I'm saying a tearful goodbye to Marco and Ivy.

"I'm so very proud of you." I hold Marco's face in my hands. "My baby boy is all grown up."

Marco quickly swipes at a stray tear. "I love you, mom. I'm really going to miss you." He wraps me in another tight hug.

"We can call and video chat anytime. And who knows, maybe I'll fly out to visit you."

"We'd love that, Liz," Ivy says as she hugs me.

"Take good care of each other."

"We will," they say in unison.

Then, it's Frannie's turn to say goodbye to her brother. Her tears are flowing freely. She can hardly speak.

"It's okay, Fran," Marco consoles his sister.

"Nothing's okay." She continues to cry.

He leans close to her and says something that only she can hear. She nods in response. I want to know what he's telling her, but over the years, I've learned that when the kids are sharing things between each other, it's no use asking. They won't tell—some sort of sibling code or something. I'm an only child, and I have no experience with this kind of relationship.

Whatever he says has calmed her. She puts her arms around his neck and squeezes him tight.

"I'm really going to miss you," Frannie says through tears.

"You and Ry can come stay with us anytime," Ivy adds. "Well, once we find a place to live."

After our goodbyes are said, Marco and Ivy leave as a couple. Francesca and Ryker leave as a couple.

I'm the only one left.

The only one without a partner.

I leave alone.

47

Elizabeth

"**I**s there anything else I need to bring?"

I'm on a video call with Grace. It's T-minus two weeks until her wedding, and she's a ball of nerves. Sefina graciously invited me to stay with them, so I've decided to fly out to Hawaii early to help Grace with last-minute wedding preparations.

"Did you get the headpiece?" Grace asks as she paces back and forth, her phone in hand.

"I did." I hold up the delicate headpiece. It looks like a thin crown of weaved flowers. The flowers are made from crystals, and the leaves are rose gold. Interwoven into the backside are long strips of lace. It's exquisite and understated.

Hawaii has been good for my daughter. As the baby of the family, I'll admit, Grace was a bit spoiled. She loved her clothes and make-up. It used to take her at least two hours to get ready to go out. Don't get me wrong. I adore my daughter. She's sweet and kind but was high maintenance. That seems to have changed—she's matured. Grace no longer lives the same way. She's no longer the girl who refuses to leave the house without hair and make-up. There's an aura of peace and tranquility about her. Makoa and his family have rubbed off on her in a very positive way.

"Thank you for agreeing to come early. I didn't want you to miss out on any of the pre-wedding traditions."

"I can't wait to get there."

How is it that my heart can be so full of happiness when I'm feeling such a significant loss at the same time? Gil and I should be doing this together. Instead, there is no Gil and me.

"Makoa and I will be at the airport to pick you up tomorrow."

Flying is not my favorite activity, and this is a thirteen-hour flight—alone.

"Thank you, sweetheart. I'm going to go and try to get a few hours of sleep before I have to leave for the airport. I'll see you tomorrow."

After we hang up, I finish packing my bag and then attempt to lay down and get some rest, but it's no use. I'm a bundle of excitement and nerves.

Frannie and Ryker offered to drive me to the airport, but I declined their invitations. My flight leaves in the middle of the night, and I didn't want them to have to be driving when they could be sleeping.

My driver drops me off at the entrance nearest my gate. With a water bottle in one hand and my carry-on luggage in the other, I make my way to the security checkpoint. Right before I cross it, I take my anxiety pill and a final drink of water before tossing the bottle in the recycling bin. With a deep breath, I approach security.

I'm early enough that I make it through the checkpoint reasonably quickly. Now I just have to wait for the boarding call.

The sedative I took knocked me out shortly after we took off. I'm woken with a gentle shake on my shoulder from the attendant.

"Ma'am, I have your meal."

A yawn escapes. "How much longer is left?"

"Just a few hours."

I'm thankful for that bit of news. I eat my meal and then read a book on my e-reader to pass the rest of the time.

Before I know it, we're approaching the airport. I reach over to grab the seatbelt and secure myself in. Now all I need to get through is the landing, and I'll be home free until I have to fly home—one step at a time Elizabeth.

We start our descent, the pilot keeps the plane steady, and then the wheels touch down. It's the smoothest landing I've ever experienced. Once we come to a complete stop, I let out the breath I was holding.

The passengers begin to file off the plane in a surprisingly orderly fashion. I'm anxious to get off and see my daughter and this beautiful island she calls paradise.

Once off the plane, I enter the bustling airport. I'm not very tall, so looking over the heads of the many travelers around me proves difficult.

"Mom, we're over here." I hear Grace's voice and see Makoa waving.

I make my way in their direction as fast as I can. When I'm close enough, Grace runs into my arms.

"I can't believe you're here," she says as she squeezes me in a hug. "I've missed you so much."

My daughter may be grown up and about to become a mother herself, but she's still my little girl. I hold her tight, so thankful to be here.

She finally let's go and Makoa steps up. "Aloha." He puts a purple and white lei around my neck. "Welcome to Hawaii."

The plumeria flowers have a sweet, fruity fragrance. "I've always wondered if getting a lei when you land in Hawaii was a real thing."

"Typically, it's something reserved for tourists from their hotels or travel agencies," Makoa explains. "My mother made this for you. She wants you to have the full Ohana experience while you're with us."

"That's very sweet of her."

"You're our family now," Makoa says proudly. "Let me take your bag, and we'll head home. Mom is preparing food for your arrival."

"I hope she didn't go through a lot of trouble."

Makoa and Grace look at each other and laugh.

"What's so funny?"

"You'll see," Grace says.

48

Elizabeth

When we leave the airport, we take the highway for a short time. Makoa takes an exit, and we make a turn onto the most beautiful road I've ever experienced. For a brief second, I feel like Anne, from Anne of Green Gables, when she's riding with Matthew to meet Marilla.

Makoa puts the top down on his Audi A5 convertible, and I get the full spectrum view.

"This is the famous Red Road," he explains.

Although it's now paved with black asphalt, Makoa tells me locals still call it by its original name. Coconut trees line the sides of the road, swaying in the tropical breeze, giving way to cliffs overlooking the cerulean blue Pacific Ocean. Occasionally the view is obscured by lush tropical rainforests whose trees and vines intertwine, creating a canopy over the road. Then, we come out of the thick brush, the views of waves crashing onto black sand shores come back into view. I don't know whether to continue taking videos and pictures or to put my phone down and absorb the ethereal beauty.

"We're home," Grace announces when Makoa makes a turn onto a dirt road.

I don't know what I'm expecting, but it isn't what I see. They live in a secluded area full of vegetation. We get out of the car and begin to walk up to a large, modern house that's surrounded by lemon, mango, coconut, and banana trees. Chickens run freely through the grass. I can hear the waves, so I know the ocean is nearby. It's truly idyllic.

Before we make it to the door, a man and woman come outside to meet us. I don't have to ask who they are. Their resemblance to Makoa is unmistakable.

"Aloha," Liko says and embraces me in a warm hug.

"Aloha, welcome to our home." Sefina kisses my cheek. "We're so glad to have you with us."

"I'm so happy to be here."

"Come inside." Sefina leads me to the door, where we slip our shoes off and enter the house. "You can get freshened up before the festivities tonight."

I don't get the chance to ask her about these festivities because I'm no longer able to speak. The house has an open and airy floor plan. The far side of the room is made entirely of windows, which open like a door. Right outside is the ocean.

Grace walks up beside me and puts her arm around me. "It's beautiful, isn't it?"

"I've never seen anything like it." The view is truly breathtaking.

"Your room faces the ocean, so you'll get to wake up to this view every morning."

"Let me show you to your room." Sefina leads me down a hallway to a door.

She opens it and motions for me to go in ahead of her. The room is painted a pale blue, mimicking the color of the sea. The bed has what looks to be a handmade quilt, complete with several fluffy pillows, and sits opposite a set of French doors that are open and lead to a private balcony.

"Your home is incredible."

"This is Makoa and Grace's home now," she says. "Liko and I are building an Ohana unit for Ke'ala and us next to this house."

Sefina explains the importance of family in their culture and how many families have multigenerational homes like this one. I'm thankful that Grace will have family so close. Being a new mother isn't easy. It's important to have that support and help, especially during those first few weeks when your body is still healing.

"I'll let you settle in. We have an exciting night ahead of us."

"What's happening tonight?"

"We're having a luau in honor of Grace's family being here and to celebrate the upcoming wedding."

With that, she exits the room, closing the door behind her.

49

Gilbert

O ur flight lands, and the three of us wait to exit the plane. "I can't believe we're in Hawaii," Frannie says. She's bouncing on her feet like a little girl.

"We need to find the rental car office," I say. "Grace said there's a car waiting for us and directions to the hotel."

"I can't wait to get there and grab a shower and then to see Grace's house," Frannie chatters as we walk through the airport. "I've seen the pictures, and it's just gorgeous."

Grace told me Makoa's parents are passing the main house on to them, but I've not had the pleasure of seeing any pictures.

"You're quiet, dad," Ryker says, putting his hand on my shoulder. "Is everything ok?"

No, nothing's okay. Liz and I always wanted to come to Hawaii. For several years we'd been saving to take an extended vacation here for our thirtieth anniversary. When we first made plans, we had no idea Grace would be going to school here, let alone living here. But now I'm here alone. Grace told me Lizzie couldn't fly out until later next week. She said there were too many orders she had to fill for the website before she's able to leave.

"I'm just tired from the long flight. Nothing a nap won't fix," I lie because I don't want my emotions to cloud the joy of the wedding.

We find the car rental office and pick up our car. Then, we put our suitcases in the trunk and get on the highway heading to our hotel.

Grace and Makoa arranged for us to stay at a resort in Honolulu. Rather than it being a hotel building, the resort is made up of a group of bungalows, all with beach access.

"I don't think I ever want to go home," Frannie exclaims as she throws open the doors and steps out onto the sand. "Ry, can we move here?"

"Funny." Ryker chuckles and follows her outside.

I sit on the bed and pull out my phone to text Grace.

(Gil) We're here. The resort is beautiful.

(Grace) Yay. I knew you'd like it.

(Gil) When should we head to your house?

(Grace) There's been a change of plans. Koa and I are going to drive up there. He knows a nice restaurant where we can have dinner.

As much as I want to see her house, I'll be here for two weeks. There's plenty of time. We've only been here a few hours, and I already feel the jetlag kicking in. Not having to drive anywhere else is okay with me.

(Gil) Sounds good. I'll let your sister and Ryker know.

(Grace) I bet she's already down at the water.

I laugh. My kids know each other so well. As I text her back, Frannie has her shoes off and is standing in the waves.

(Gil) You'd be right.

(Grace) I'll text you when we're almost there.

I debate taking a nap or joining the kids down at the water and decide to go outside with them. I want to get some pictures of these first moments. Frannie may be fully grown, but she's still my daughter, and she's experiencing a first.

With my cell phone in hand, I snap pictures and take videos as I make my way through the sand down to the water.

50

Elizabeth

There's a knock on my door.

"Come in," I call.

"Are you ready to go?" Grace asks

"Almost. I'm not sure what to wear to a luau."

Grace comes over to where I have several outfits laid out on the bed. She doesn't waste time picking up a light pink strapless dress.

"This'll be perfect." She holds it up.

"Don't you think it's a bit too much?" I was thinking more of a pair of shorts and a flowy shirt."Not at all. You'll fit right in." She smiles.

I look at her and realize she's wearing a similar dress. Grace's is a floral print ankle-length dress with spaghetti straps. She has her hair pulled half back with little braids.

"You're glowing. Pregnancy suits you."

"I'm so happy here now," she says and sits on the bed. "I was so close to coming home until I met Koa. He changed everything."

"You really love him."

"I know it probably sounds crazy. I've only known him for six months, but he's my soul mate."

Grace can't contain the smile on her face when she talks about her fiancé.

"It's not crazy at all." I sit next to her. "The heart knows when it's met its mate. I just wish your father would remember that feeling."

Grace pops up quickly. "If we don't get going, we're going to be late."

"Where are we going?"

"The luau is at a restaurant in Honolulu. I'll leave you to get changed."

I change my clothes and debate whether to pull my hair back or leave it down. I decide to throw an elastic in my purse just in case I need to pull it back later.

When I get back to the main room, Grace and Makoa are waiting for me there.

"Sorry I took so long."

"We have plenty of time," Makoa reassures me. "My parents and sister left a few minutes ago. We'll meet them there."

We get back into his convertible an,d begin the drive back up to Honolulu with the top down.

We pull into the parking lot of a beachfront resort.

"Is this where the luau is?" I ask.

"Yes. Many of the resorts here host them," Makoa explains. "Friends of my parents own this resort."

"That makes sense."

We get out of the car and walk down a path leading to several beachfront bungalows. I can see what appears to be tiki torches and a small gathering of people on the beach near the water.

"I need to use the bathroom before we go down to the water," Grace says. "Do you mind walking with me, Mom?"

"Not at all."

"Are you two ladies okay if I head down?"

"Sure." Grace stands on her tiptoes and places a kiss on Makoa's lips. "We'll be there in a few minutes."

Makoa heads down to the water while we head to one of the bungalows. There are lights on in it.

"Are you sure this is the right one? It looks like someone's staying in here."

"Yes. The owners gave us a key and told us they'd leave the lights on so we had access to a bathroom. She has five children of her own." Grace laughs nervously and puts her hand on her tummy.

When we get to the door, Grace swipes her key card, the green light comes on, and we walk in. I'm immediately concerned because there're someone's personal belongings in here. "I think we're in the wrong place," I whisper, not wanting to get caught or scare whoever's room we just invaded. "Come on, let's go." I grab her arm, but she doesn't move.

"Grace, is that you?"

Before I can say anything, Gilbert walks into the room.

"Liz?" he asks and looks between Grace and me.

"Grace, what's going on?"

Francesca and Ryker come from the same hallway Gil just emerged from.

"Hi, mom," Fran says.

The door to the bungalow opens, startling me. Hunter walks in, followed by Emerie and Makoa.

"What's going on here?" I ask.

"I'd like an answer to that as well," Gil says.

We're staging an intervention," Grace says. "You and Dad need to talk to each other."

"There's nothing to be said." I turn to walk to the door, but Makoa beats me to it and blocks my exit. "Really?"

Makoa crosses his arms and smiles.

"When we were growing up, you and dad taught us how to handle our disagreements," Hunter says.

"And ignoring each other wasn't part of it."

"Marco?"

Hunter holds up his phone, and I see Marco's face on a video chat.

"You always told us we couldn't run from our problems or ignore them," Marco continues.

"You drilled into us to never go to bed angry with someone." Frannie chimes in.

"This is different," I explain. "What you father did—"

Hunter holds up his hand. "You have no idea what dad did or didn't do because you refuse to talk to him." He turns to his father. "And you've been too stubborn to try to explain it to mom unless she talked to you in person."

"So, now you two are face-to-face," Grace says. "And it's our turn to be the adults."

"What are you talking about," Gil asks.

"Do you remember when we were little, and we'd fight with each other?" Frannie asks.

"Yes," Gil responds.

"You'd put us in our rooms and tell us we couldn't come out until we talked it through and made up."

"Well, that's what we're doing," Grace says, hands on her hips.

"You can't be serious. We're the parents here, not the children."

"It's time to start acting like it," Marco says.

The group of them moves to the door.

"We're going down to the luau. You and dad are staying here to work this out." Grace waves her hand in front of her. "I don't care if it takes days we've got time."

"And don't worry, dad," Frannie says. "Ryker and I aren't staying in this bungalow. You and mom have it all to yourselves."

They grab their bags off the sofa.

"And how do you plan on keeping us in here?" I ask.

Makoa opens the door, and standing outside are two huge, very scary-looking men.

"With them." He smiles.

"When you two talk this through and makeup, text one of us, and we'll be back," Hunter says.

And just like that, the kids file out of the room, closing the door behind them.

I turn and face Gil.

"You better not have had anything to do with this."

51

Gilbert

"I had no idea they were planning this," I say. "Grace told me you weren't flying in until next week."

"She told me the same thing about you."

There's a knock on the door.

I move to answer it, and Liz takes a large step to the side.

"Here's your dinner." One of the men pushes a cart with two plates covered with cloches through the doorway before promptly going back out, closing the door behind them. I lift one of the lids to see what smells so good. The offerings on the plate are colorful. Artfully arranged on taro leaves are preparations of pork and salmon. There are purple potatoes with shredded coconut on top and neatly placed scoops of rice—my mouth waters looking at the delicious food.

"Hungry?" I ask Liz.

"I was, but I've suddenly lost my appetite."

"I'll put this aside for later then." With a bit of disappointment, I push the cart into the kitchenette area and then sit on the wicker sofa. "You may as well get comfortable. I don't think we're getting out of here any time soon."

Liz rolls her eyes before she sits on the opposite side of the couch and crosses her arms.

They say silence is deafening. I never fully understood that until right now. Liz and I sit in the same room, and although no audible words have been spoken, every thought and emotion silently projected is louder than anything I've ever experienced.

So many thoughts race through my mind. One of which is shock at what our kids have managed to pull off. I know it shouldn't surprise me. Our fabulous four are tight. When they put their minds to something, they rarely fail. This is by far the most critical mission they've ever attempted—they've managed to get Liz and me in the same room together. How this will turn out is still anyone's guess, but I'm not giving up without a fight.

This may be my only chance to talk to Liz. To force her to listen to me.

Here goes nothing. "I know you think you know what you saw."

Liz turns to face me anger pulses off her in waves. "I don't think I know. I'm certain I know."

"And what are you so certain you saw?"

"You being physical with another woman."

"Do you think I'd cheat on you?"

She knows what she means to me. She has to know. I've never given her reason to doubt me. That's what hurts so much—that she'd ever doubt my faithfulness.

"I never thought you would." She uncrosses her arms, her shoulders fall. "Until I saw it."

"Liz." I try to move closer to her, but she puts her hand up, stopping me. "I did not kiss Camila."

"You must think I'm stupid." Her face reddens with anger.

"I do not think you're stupid."

"That's debatable." She sighs loudly.

"It's the truth."

Liz stands and walks toward the window. "The first time I met Camila, you remember, at the office Christmas party?"

I nod.

"There was something about her. She was too familiar with you—her body language and the way she spoke to you. It made me uncomfortable. I didn't like her, and she clearly didn't like me. After the party, I tried to tell you that she was interested in you as more than her boss. You said she was just young and excited about her new job."

"And I didn't believe you."

As she talks about that night, I'm brought back to our karaoke date and how I felt when Liz was on the stage with that college kid. They sang a song that, at least in the movie, was a romantic ballad between a couple. I was able to manage that part because it was just an act on the stage, but when he walked her back to the table and asked her to get drinks with him, it took everything in me not to hit him—and I'm not a violent man. Just the mere thought that another man, no matter how much younger than her he was, was interested in my wife was more than I could handle.

In that case, that was a kid we'd never see again, so it was easy to get over it. But for Liz, Camila is someone she has to deal with every day. For the first time, I understand Liz's anguish, and it's crushing. I don't know what I would've done if it had been me walking in seeing another man kiss Liz. Would I have reacted the same way? That's an easy answer, no. I would've done much worse.

Guilt hits me hard. For the past few months, I've been walking around playing the role of victim. I've believed Liz's actions were over the top and unreasonable. But now that I've taken a minute to see things through her eyes, things look very different.

Liz walks toward me and stops at the back of the couch. "I hoped my plan of showing up for lunch that day would send a clear message to her that you were off-limits, but either she didn't get the hint, or you two had something going on all along."

"That's not fair." I get up and circle the couch to stand in front of her. "I thought she got the hint too. Obviously, we were both wrong."

"Then." Liz pokes her finger in my chest. "You had the nerve to bring her to our home."

The pain in my wife's eyes is almost unbearable. I struggle not to look away.

"Looking back, I see what a bad decision that was." I try to touch her hand, but she pulls it away. "My only thought was getting to spend my lunchtime with you."

"You allowed her to come into our home," she reiterates. "My safe place. And she attacked me. The things she said, the way she made me feel. And then to see you two—" Liz begins crying.

52

Elizabeth

"And her unbuttoned shirt? How do you plan to explain that?"

"She was holding a file against her chest. I don't pay her that much attention."

"Convenient."

I don't want to cry or show weakness, but my tears betray me and fall anyway. In my mind, the picture is so clear. Camila's blouse was open. Her hands were threaded through his hair. He was holding her arms.

"Your lips—you were kissing her. It's obvious I walked in right before you—"

My stomach churns, and I'm unable to control the nausea that's bubbling inside. I jump up and rush to the bathroom. I drop to my knees and empty what little is in my stomach into the toilet. Gil is right on my heels and holds my hair back.

"Go away, please."

"I'm not going anywhere, Liz," he says and continues to hold my hair back.

My body continues retching.

"We're a couple, a team." He rubs my back, trying to soothe me. "I haven't given up on us, and I'm begging you not to give up either."

My body finally stills, and I slide back to lean against the wall.

Gil goes to the sink and wets a cloth with cool water. Then, he kneels next to me and tenderly wipes my face. His honey-colored eyes meet mine. I can see his pain as well as his resolve reflected in his gaze.

"I'm not signing the divorce papers," he says softly.

"You cheated on me."

"No, Liz. I didn't," he insists. He gets up and tosses the washcloth back in the sink. "Are you okay to stand up?"

"I think so." Gil offers me his hand, and I tentatively reach out, allowing him to help me.

"Let's talk, please."

I can choose to be stubborn, like I've been, and refuse to talk to him. But what good will that do? Our kids have literally stationed guards outside the door. I need to suck up my pride and get this conversation over with so we can begin moving on.

Gil leads me back to the main room, where I sit on the couch. He makes his way into the kitchen. I watch as he opens the small refrigerator and takes out two water bottles before coming to sit. He passes one to me.

"Thank you." I open it and take a sip of the refreshingly cold water.

"We need to start from square one," Gil says. "Then we can go step by step until we work this out."

That comment is so Gil. Even in this, he's patterned and organized. In my opinion, we can break it down however he'd like, but what's done is done. There's no coming back from infidelity. I screw the cap onto the water bottle and set it down on the small table next to the sofa.

"I see the look on your face. You're shutting me out already." This man knows me too well. "Don't you think you owe it to us—" He gestures between him and me. "To at least have an honest conversation?"

I'm not seeing a path where we come out as a couple. But I guess we both deserve the opportunity to be heard. Maybe it'll help us to move on.

"Fine." I concede. "We can talk, but I'm not making any promises. I filed for divorce. There's no amount of talking that will change that."

"I'll meet you halfway," Gil concedes. "If, after we talk, you still feel the same way, I'll sign the papers."

I'm shocked that Gil is compromising. It's usually all or nothing. There's no gray area in his mind.

"You go first," he says.

"That woman." I ball my hands into fists. "That night at the Christmas party. I tried to tell you she was trouble. I'm your wife." My hand covers my heart that feels like it's splitting in two. "It felt like you weren't listening to me, blowing me off. Siding with her."

"You said you didn't like her, that you got a bad feeling about her. But she didn't do anything wrong. I didn't understand why."

"Why?" The words spill from my mouth. "Camila didn't know I was in the restroom when she came in with one of her friends. Camila talked about how hot her boss was and how she felt bad for him being married to a fat woman. They laughed and talked about how easy it would be for her to get you in bed."

I was a coward that night, unable to face her. I hid in the stall and waited until they left before I came out. It took everything I had to keep the tears back and step out into the party.

"Why didn't you tell me?"

"Would you have taken it seriously or just brushed it off as silly girl talk?" I know my question is going to sting, but, at this point, we're too far gone to worry about being careful with my words. I've held these feelings in for too long. I tried to be friendly and look at where it's gotten me.

"You're probably right," he admits.

"You always try to see the best in people. To a fault."

That's something I've always loved about Gil, his ability to find something positive in almost any situation. He's never had trouble making and keeping friends. In this situation, I don't know if he's refusing to see or really can't see Camila for exactly what she is.

"I honestly don't get it, Liz. She never did anything, never tried to hit on me," Gil argues. "I guess that's what I didn't understand back then. And why I don't understand how things escalated to this point."

You're serious, aren't you?"

Gil scrunches his forehead and nods.

"For the past year, she's been silently throwing herself at you. Take the way she dresses. She's not the only woman in your department. How do the other women dress?"

His head tilts as he thinks about it. "Mostly jeans or pants of some kind, I guess." He shrugs. "I really don't pay attention."

"Exactly, they wear clothes appropriate for their line of work. But Camila chooses short, tight skirts and heels. That's hardly ideal for a housing inspector." "I never thought about it," Gil admits.

And that's a part of the problem. Since we started dating, Gil never noticed if a girl was batting her eyes at him or flirting. Because of that, I either had to try to ignore their advances or be the bad guy and take care of it on my own. When we were younger, that was fine. Teenage girls can be fickle. If the boy doesn't pay attention or his girl chases them off, they move on fairly quickly.

But adult women, that's a different story. Camila has been laser-focused on my husband. My warnings and demonstrations of possession didn't cut it. Women like her need to see a united front—they need their target to step up and speak out.

"I figured it was best not to make a big deal about it—even though I wasn't sure what it was," Gil says. "Obviously, I was wrong. But to be honest, Liz, I still don't understand what I was supposed to do."

"You should've confronted her. Told her, in no uncertain terms, that you weren't interested." My voice gets louder. I don't want to end up in a screaming match, so I stop and take a few deep breaths to calm myself. "Instead, I felt alone. Like I was the only one standing up for me—for us. It didn't work, though. She didn't take me seriously because I didn't have you backing me up."

"Of course, I backed you up."

"Exactly how did you back me up?"

"On the nights we had to stay late to correct her mistakes, she'd ask me to go to dinner with her when we were finished, and I always told her no."

"She asked you to dinner?" I yell.

"It was just a polite invitation, you know, out of obligation because of having to stay late."

I growl in frustration. This is precisely what I'm talking about. He thinks her dinner invite was just a kind gesture or an obligatory invite. Why can't he see it for what it was? I want to scream or shake him—anything to get through to him.

"Gil, one of the things I've always loved about you is how kind you are. But in this case, your kindness is misplaced." I've been holding back my suspicions about her errors, but no more. I'm putting all my cards on the table. "I don't think her mistakes were innocent. I think she was purposely making errors because she knew she'd get to be alone with you."

Gil's amber eyes grow dark with anger.

"Liz—"

"Hear me out." I hold up my hand. "Camila's worked in your department for around a year. You trained her. She manages to get the paperwork right when she's paired up with anyone else in the office. But when she's paired with you, that same paperwork gets so screwed up it takes hours to fix."

I stop and give him a few minutes to process what I've just said.

Gil's quiet, but I can tell he's thinking. I know the moment he gets it because his shoulders fall.

"None of that ever crossed my mind. I thought she was just struggling with the job."

"That's because you're a good man. You have a good heart. Sadly, not everyone is like that."

53

Gilbert

My wife is right. Camila has been hitting on me or at least trying to, and I did nothing about it. What's wrong with me? It makes me feel like less of a man that my wife has to explain these things to me. But, I'm finally starting to see things through Liz's eyes, and I don't like what I see. I'm just hoping my realization hasn't come too late.

"Why didn't Camila back off after you came into the office that day?" I ask not to argue, but because I genuinely don't understand.

"Because we didn't have a united front." Liz sounds exasperated. "I made a stand for us, but you stood silent on the sidelines. You didn't stand up for us."

I sit back and close my eyes. Guilt hits me hard because she's right. I didn't do my part to stop her. I let this happen.

Instead of protecting my wife, the dearest person in my life, I kept putting her, albeit unintentionally, in the line of fire. I invited Camila into my home, where she verbally attacked Elizabeth.

On my watch, Camila took my wife's deepest insecurities and used them against her. She called her washed up, which couldn't be further from the truth.

I know Liz doesn't see herself as attractive. She works out every day and barely eats because she doesn't like her body. Strewn across her dresser are creams to tighten her skin, get rid of her wrinkles, and hide her stretch marks. Every six weeks, she sees her stylist to color her grays so she doesn't look old.

But when I look at Liz, I only see my breathtaking wife. Her physical body is curvy and attractive. The stretch marks she hates so much only remind me of how her body carried the four lives we created together. Things she considers signs of aging that she feels must be hidden; are nothing to be ashamed of. Our physical bodies age, no one can avoid that, but I don't see it as detracting from her beauty. Every day I wake up and thank God that this smart, patient, beautiful woman chose me. There's nothing and no one that will ever change that.

Camila tried. She used my wife's insecurities, things I find the most beautiful, to hurt her—to cause a rift between us.

"I'm glad you finally realize all this, but it's too little too late," Liz says quietly.

"It can't be too late."

Now, it's my turn to let my doubts and insecurities spill.

"We were really growing closer?"

"What does that mean?"

"All the dates. Were they real, or were they just to grow the website?"

There. I said it. At first, the dates were great. They felt authentic. Liz and I were finally at a place where we could focus on each other. But then it felt like there was a shift. That the dates were more about research for the website and less about us. I began to wonder if I was enough. Would Liz still want to explore all these dating scenarios with me if there was no Real Life Romance?

"You were so excited about the website, so I kept the doubts to myself," I explain.

"First, you say it's not too late. Now you question if our reconnecting was real?"

"I'm telling you my fears. Things that are bothering me," I explain. "Isn't that what you did?

"All this time, you thought our dates were only about the website?"

"Not at first." It's hard to say this aloud, but if we have any hope of moving past this moment in time, we need to be completely honest with each other about everything. "But after a while, it felt like the website overshadowed us. Like we were only going out as research, rather than connection."

I tried to be careful with my words, but I can see they still hurt. But I have to know.

"Yes, we used the dates for the website, but what I felt had nothing to do with the site. I thought we were growing closer, but

I was wrong. You just made that clear." Liz's words are clipped. "That explains why the minute we had a serious fight, you ran right to her."

"No, Liz. It's not like that." I scrub my hands down my face. "Questioning the intention behind our dates did not drive me into another woman's arms."

I have so many questions about that afternoon. Camila kept making excuses to come into my office. Quite frankly, she was driving me crazy, interrupting me all morning. The timing of it all was too perfect. It's almost like she knew Liz was planning to come in, but that's impossible. She wasn't on the schedule.

Wait a minute...

"Did you happen to call the office that day?""Why?"

I can feel my body temperature rising as my anxiety level grows. "Did you call?"

"Yes. I was hoping to ask Liam what your schedule was."

"He had the day off."

"I found that out when Camila answered."

Camila isn't supposed to be answering Liam's line. But with this information, things are beginning to make sense.

"Did she know you were coming in?""Kind of." Liz shrugs. "She asked if I wanted to leave a message, but I told her I'd tell you when I came in."

I jump up from the couch. "She knew you were coming—Camila set us up."

"I didn't tell her when or even if I was coming."

Clearly, Liz isn't as convinced as me."We've already established that Camila is sneaky. She took a calculated risk, and it worked in her favor."

Yet again, Camila shouldn't have been in my office, and for at least the tenth time that day, I told her that, but she insisted she had a file I needed to review. She was holding it against her chest, which is why I didn't notice her blouse unbuttoned. Then, everything happened so fast. Before I knew it, Liz was running out of my office.

"Camila timed it perfectly, so you'd walk in and see her kissing me. But you ran out before I could explain."

"I wasn't sticking around to see what came next."

"As your husband, I think I at least deserved to be heard." I sit next to Liz and take her hand in mine. "Because I could've told you that my hands were on her arms to push her away. To tell her she had no right to kiss me and that her sexual advances were unwanted."

"Gil—""It's my turn to talk," I interrupt. "I was blindsided by what Camila did. I know you tried to warn me, but I didn't see it until it went too far. You were hurt on my watch." I hit my chest. "I'm sorry, Liz. Words don't fix anything. I get it. But I need you to know how much I truly regret my mistakes and how they affected you. I also want you to know I went to Tessa Langley."

54

Elizabeth

At first, I wasn't buying Gil's story. He didn't think our dates were real? That they were just research for the website. But then I heard the genuine pain in his voice. And when he started questioning me about that fateful afternoon, the pieces began to fall into place.

That's when I realized how wrong I was. How terribly I've behaved.

With guilt weighing heavy on my chest, I can hardly breathe; I listen as Gil tells me the rest of the story.

"Tessa asked me to be patient and keep quiet about the incident until she got back to me," he explains. "I was beginning to think she forgot or wasn't going to do anything when she called me to her office."

Gil takes his time explaining each step of the meeting in detail. How Tessa received multiple complaints about Camila's inappropriate behavior regarding Gil in the office. The problem was unless he filed a complaint, there was nothing Tessa could do. Then, he laid out the options Tessa presented.

"I apologize if you're upset that I gave my consent for Camila getting a second chance rather than losing her job."

I'm mad—furious. I want to stomp my feet and yell that he should've let her get fired. But I can't. That move is classic Gilbert, and it's what made me fall in love with him when we met, and it's what continued to make me fall for him every day since.

"She'll be in Charlene's office across town. Our paths will not cross. It's her last chance. If there's even one more complaint against her, she'll be fired on the spot."

With that, he becomes quiet. He watches me, searching my face for any clue as to what I may be thinking but never letting go of my hands.

"And the past few months, the phone calls, letters, and all the flowers." I let a smile slip. "You could've left the explanation on a voicemail or written in it a letter. Why didn't you?"

"The kids kept telling me the same thing—that I should've told you in any way I could." Gil shrugs. "But I needed you to hear it from me, not read it or listen to a voicemail. It wouldn't have been the same."

I laugh. "I've been told the same thing. They kept begging me to pick up the phone. Hunter even offered to come up from Florida to drive me to Chris's apartment, so we could talk."

"So, now what?" Gil asks, uncertain.Walking over to the window, I look at the luau that's underway. Tiki torches burn bright, their flames dance as though they're part of the festivities. Men and women, dressed in native clothes, tell ancient stories through their graceful dance movements around the bonfire. The hypnotic drum beat floats on the breeze. Our family is enjoying the celebration, seemingly oblivious to what's going on inside the bungalow.

Now what? That's a very good question. I feel foolish for ignoring Gilbert the past few months. I allowed pride to get in the way and broke one of the vows we made to each other at our wedding—I'll always be willing to listen without judgment and will never go to bed angry.We lived by those vows for twenty-seven years. They've served us well. Have we had arguments? Sure, I don't know a couple who hasn't. Looking back, most of them were about trivial things. Heck, many times after arguing for hours, we didn't even remember what we were initially mad about. We'd laugh, apologize, and make up.

What was different this time? It's clear that no matter how many years a couple's together, problems can still arise and get blown out of proportion. I think that's the issue we need to address.

I turn around to face Gil. "This all started because we were arguing about Grace getting married. We stopped communicating with each other. Then, I assumed you ran to

Camila. That you chose her over me." I drop my head. "I messed up."

"I'm at fault in this too," Gil admits. "When Grace and Makoa told us that not only did they want to get married, but that she was pregnant, my head was ready to explode. I couldn't think straight. My emotions were so overwhelming I was unable to find the words to adequately express what I was feeling. But instead of taking a few minutes to calm down and find the words, I let anger take over. I was wrong, and I'm sorry."

"I forgive you." I look out the window once more. "But I think there are two other people who deserve an apology."

"I've already taken care of that. Before I got on the plane to come here, Makoa and I had a conversation where he allowed me the space to express my concerns. He addressed each one. He's a good man, and he loves Grace. I see that now." Gil walks over to me. "Before I got on the plane, the three of us had a long video chat. I apologized and gave them my blessing."

I guess that leaves us now.

After finally getting past my anger and stubbornness and listening to my husband, I realize how wrong I was. Admitting fault is never easy, but if there's to be a future for Gil and me, and I want there to be, it's what I have to do.

"I'm sorry. I was wrong to jump to conclusions and even more wrong to shut you out."

"Lizzie, I love you. No woman can hold a candle to you." With his finger, he lifts my chin, so my eyes meet his. "You're everything to me."

Tears fall once again. This time they're a mixture of regret, embarrassment, and happiness. So many intertwined emotions rush through me.

"I love you, Gil. I'm so sorry for my behavior. Can you forgive me?"

"I already have."

He opens his arms to me, and I allow myself to fall into them. I rest my head on his chest as he holds me tight.

For the first time in months, everything feels right.

Pulling back, I ask. "Do you have the divorce papers with you?"

"I do." The hopeful look that was just on his face is now replaced with sadness. "I'll go get them."

It takes a few minutes, but finally, he comes back with the papers and a pen in his hand.

"I promised if you still wanted, I'd sign these after we talked." He sets the papers on the table and clicks his pen to sign. "I thought maybe you'd changed your mind, but I accept your decision."

Gil flips to the last page and begins to sign, but I interrupt him. "I think it's best if we rip those up."

"Really?" His voice cracks with emotion.

I nod.

"Do you want to do the honors?" He holds the papers out to me.

I take them and tear them in half. As I continue to tear, allowing small pieces of paper to flutter to the floor, the broken fragments of our relationship begin to put themselves back together. I keep ripping until there's nothing but a pile of worthless scraps of paper scattered in tiny pieces by my feet.

I take slow steps toward my husband. When he looks at me, I see desire reflected in his gaze.

"So, now what?" I ask quietly.

Without answering, he takes my hand and leads me down the hall to the bedroom.

We spend the rest of the night making up.

55

Gilbert

Liz is asleep in my arms, something I never thought would happen again. My cell phone pings, and I carefully reach over to the nightstand where I left it last night.

(Hunter) Good morning. Just checking to make sure you're both alive.

(Gil) We are.

(Hunter) Are you two still fighting?

I look at the woman lying next to me, her black hair spilling over her pillow. She's an angel—my angel.

(Gil) I think it's safe to say we've made up.

(Hunter) Perfect. I'm sending our security home.

(Gil) They're still there?

(Hunter) They are.

I can't believe those men stayed outside the door all night.

(Hunter) We're all on our way over.

(Gil) Um...that's not a good idea.

(Hunter) Say no more.

I chuckle. Hunter still hasn't fully recovered from walking in on us on the couch.

(Gil) We'll come find you kids later.

Liz stirs next to me and pushes up on her elbow. "Who are you talking to?""Hunter. The kids wanted to come over."

"I guess we need to get up and get dressed," she says, disappointment in her voice.

I grab her hand. "You'll do no such thing. I told them we'd find them later." I kiss her. "I need more time alone with my wife."

"I see," she says.

Then, I tenderly and slowly pour all my love into her.

56

Elizabeth

The past two weeks have flown by. Hawaii is paradise. Grace and her siblings took over the last-minute wedding preparations so Gil and I could have a second honeymoon at the resort. We've enjoyed carefree days lounging on the beach and romantic nights alone in our bungalow.

Tomorrow our little girl is getting married. It's exciting and bittersweet. Buy today, Grace and Makoa have opted to spend the day apart, each with their own family. Then tonight, we'll all come together for dinner.

Grace planned a day out on the water for us. Two of her co-workers are taking us, by boat, to Shark's Cove to do some snorkeling. Initially, Gil freaked out. He loves being on the shore but isn't a huge fan of swimming in the home of so many sea creatures, especially sharks. Grace assured him that there are no sharks there—or at least there usually aren't. But it's the ocean and has some degree of unpredictability.

After packing our bags for the day, we make our way to the marina, where we're introduced to Kaia and Adrien, who are waiting for us on the boat. The kids tell Gil and me to get on board first while they giggle and whisper behind us.

"What are they up to now?"

"I haven't a clue." He shrugs.

Once we're safely onboard, Grace gives us a tour of the very impressive yacht that's owned by Makoa's parents, who've graciously allowed us to take it out for the day.

She leads us up a set of steps giving us a tour of the living quarters. There's a massive kitchen with all high-end appliances. It would be any chef's dream. Then we see the entertainment area where there's a plush sofa and several chairs arranged by a fireplace. Above the fireplace is a flatscreen TV. As we keep walking, we exit through a set of glass doors onto the deck, where there's a hot tub.

"This is incredible."

"Makoa's parents are very successful," Grace says. "They're also generous, which is why good fortune returns to them."

She takes us up another set of steps.

"This level holds all the staterooms." Grace points to a door. "You and dad need to check out the master stateroom. It's unbelievable."

Gil and I walk down the corridor. He reaches for the handle and pushes the door open.

"What?" I put my hands over my mouth. "I don't believe this."

Liam, Marco, and Ivy are standing in the room, each with a giant grin on their face.

"What are you all doing here?" Gil asks.

"You didn't think I'd miss my sister's wedding, did you?"

I don't care how or why. I'm thrilled to have all my children together for this occasion.

"I'll admit, you pulled one over on us this time," Gil says. "Although this was good. Please promise no more surprises, at least for a little while."

"Well," Marco hesitates. "We may have one more."

"Don't tell me you and Ivy got married?" He laughs.

"Actually, we did."

Gil looks at me, his eyes wide and his face pale. For a second, I think he might pass out. But the only thing I can do is laugh. Our kids never cease to amaze me. Once again, they've proven they're capable of the most over-the-top surprises.

"When did you do that?" Gil asks, exasperated.

"We had a few extra days before we were expected to be in Japan, so we decided to spend a few days in Vegas," Ivy says, then looks at Marco and smiles. "Marco knows how much I love Paris, so when we found out we could get married in the Eiffel Tower, we couldn't resist. It was a spur-of-the-moment decision."

"Who else knew about this?" Gil asks and looks around at the myriad of guilty faces.

"I'm the only one." Liam sheepishly raises his hand. "Am I fired now?"

"The jury's still out on that," Gil jokes.

"Congratulations, you two." I give my son and my new daughter-in-law a hug. "I'm so happy for you." I turn back to Gil. "Just think of all the grandkids we're hopefully going to have soon."

Gil tries to keep a straight face, but it's no use. He gives in to the moment and begins laughing. "I hope you at least got pictures."

"Lots." Ivy beams.

Adrien sticks his head in the room. "Are we ready to sail?"

After a resounding yes, we follow him down to the outdoor deck. Little by little, the view of the marina disappears and is replaced by crystal clear water that appears to sparkle beneath the cloudless azure sky. I don't think we could've picked a more perfect day to be out on the ocean.

While we sail, we spot a pod of dolphins that swim right up to the boat. These amazing animals give us quite the show as they swim and splash in the wake of the boat before moving on.

We finally arrive at Shark's Cove. The water is so calm it's hard to believe it's part of the ocean. Adrien drops the anchor and gives those of us who don't know how to use a snorkel some basic directions. Once everyone's in their swimsuits, Adrien flips a switch, and a swim deck begins to slide out from the back of the boat.

One by one, everyone jumps into the water, eager to go on their swim adventure. We spend a delightful afternoon swimming with some of the most beautiful fish I've ever laid eyes on. There are Tangs, Surgeonfish, Butterfly Fish, and we're even treated to a visit from a sea turtle.

Even better than the ocean life that we spent the day with is the fact that our family is all together.

We head back to land just as the sun is beginning to set.

57

Gilbert

Swimming in a place called Shark's Cove was not exactly my idea of a fun afternoon. I had visions of being eaten by a Great White. Thankfully, we haven't seen a single shark, only schools of what appears to be friendly marine life. It's an afternoon well-deserved after the past few months.

When we're done swimming, Liz and I sit on the boat deck and watch the kids who are still snorkeling and exploring the cove. Liz is taking videos and pictures while I get lost in my thoughts. My family is growing and changing—whether I like it or not. I need to do a better job of being like the waves in the sea. They form in a rhythmic rise and fall. Some are bigger than others and crash with fury. Others are soft and calm. No matter the size or strength of the wave, each comes and goes. It's a reminder to me that nothing in life lasts forever.

My children, who were once young and dependent on me, are now adults capable of caring for themselves. Does that mean they don't need me? No. My role in their life has merely shifted, like the sand as the waves recede into the sea. But just as the next wave will reach the shore to meet the sand, my children will always come back, and I'll always be there for them.

After our day on the boat is done, we gather at an oceanfront restaurant to celebrate the joining of our families tomorrow.

Liko's seated at the head of the table on one side, and I'm seated at the head of the table on the opposite side. I take a minute to soak in the scene in front of me—two families about to become one. Everyone is eating, talking, and laughing.

By my side is my radiant wife. She grasps my hand, and I give it a little squeeze. I don't know what I did to deserve this woman, but I guarantee I won't do anything to jeopardize losing her again.

For me, today was about so much more than making lasting family memories. My eyes were opened to an important lesson about life. It's a day I'll not forget.

After dinner's finished, everyone says their goodbyes. Grace is spending the night with Francesca, Ivy, Emerie, and Ke'ala while the boys all go to Makoa's house. Liz and I return to our bungalow.

"I have an idea I want to run by you." It's something I've been thinking about over the past few weeks but have been apprehensive to bring up.

"What is it?"

"There's a box I'd like us to make for the website."

She lowers the book to her lap. "I wasn't sure you'd want to keep doing the website."

"Why not?"

"After what you said, I assumed you'd want to close the site." She grabs her bookmark to save her spot and puts the book on the nightstand giving me her full attention. "What's your idea?" "I'd like to do a how-to fight fair box."

Liz raises her eyebrows and stares at me for what feels like forever.

"You're serious?"

"Very."

Liz and I have been together since we were sixteen years old. We've been married twenty-seven years, and still, one fight nearly broke us. We've both learned and have grown from the experience. I think we should share what we've learned with other couples. Maybe we can spare someone from going through the same thing.

The box would contain all the tools a couple would need to fight fair. To ensure they're able to have their voice heard as well as to teach good hearing skills. Listening is easy. Anyone can listen, but actually hearing the other person is an entirely different thing.

"I don't think many people know how to fight in a productive way," I explain. "Perhaps if there are ground rules set ahead of time, it'll help couples when they have that big fight because everyone is going to have it."

She bites her lip. "You know, I think that's a perfect idea."

I grab the resort's stationery and pen and climb onto the bed next to Liz while brainstorming ideas for the box.

58

Elizabeth

I'm shocked listening to Gil tell me he wants to make a new box for Real Life Romance. After he told me how he felt on our dates, I didn't think this was something he'd want to pursue any further. I can't lie. I'm glad he does. I enjoy the site, and our customers like it too. I also think his idea for a how-to fight box is genius.

"One thing I think is important is to provide suggestions for how to communicate."

"What do you mean?" Gil asks.

"Everyone has a communication method that's easier for them," I explain. "Verbal communication is the best, but if someone is struggling with it, they need an alternative way to express themselves."

"I didn't think about that. We'll start with communication methods."

Gil and I make a list of different ways couples can communicate with each other because, as we've learned, the pain and anger only grow bigger if communication stops.

After we develop a good list, we move to ground rules.

"I think there should be a cool-down time where the couple doesn't have to talk to one another," I suggest.

"That sounds like giving the silent treatment. Don't you think that's dangerous?"

"It's to avoid the silent treatment or the refusal to talk to your partner for months." She looks down.

"What happened is behind us." I use my finger to lift her chin. "We can put this in place for us too. For next time."

"I hope there isn't a next time, but that sounds like a good idea."

For this box, we explain why we feel having a cool-down time is essential but that there must be a set end to it. If not, this brief time-out can turn into months where you shut each other out—something that's not healthy for any relationship. We suggest a few different lengths of time for the box, and we agree on a twenty-minute cool-down period for us.

It takes a few hours before we have everything we want outlined for the box. When I look at the clock, I'm shocked.

"Gil, it's two a.m. We need to get some sleep, or we're never going to survive tomorrow."

He puts the notepad and pen on the nightstand. "Time flies when you're having fun, I guess."

Gil sets his alarm clock, yes, he brought his trusty clock radio from home, and I set the alarm on my phone, just in case. Then, we crawl under the blankets. I cuddle up by Gil's side, my head on his chest as I drift off to sleep.

59

Elizabeth

I take a quick shower before throwing a sundress on. Grace texted about fifteen minutes ago that they'd be here to pick me up shortly. We're all heading to the wedding venue to get ready for the ceremony.

"Liz, are you ready?" Gil yells down the hall. "The girls are outside."

"Be right there."

Going through my suitcase, I grab the wrapped box containing Grace's wedding gift and head into the main room. Gil's waiting there for me.

"Mrs. Benton, you're as beautiful as the day I married you." He walks over and puts his arms around my waist, pulling me close to him.

"And you, Mr. Benton, are just as handsome as the day I married you."

"There's never been a prettier mother-of-the-bride."

Compliments are difficult for me to accept. It's something I'm working on because I know it's important to Gil.

"Thank you," I say and kiss him. "I'll see you later."

The boys are coming to pick him up, but they overslept and are running late.

I make my way out to the waiting car, where the four girls are giggling like school children.

"Do you mind if I crash the party?" I say as I get in.

"I'm getting married today," Grace squeals and wraps her arms around my neck.

"You aren't excited, are you?" I chuckle.

"She was up all night." Emerie yawns.

Francesca laughs. "I had to threaten to smother her with a pillow to get her to go to sleep."

The girls chatter nonstop on the short drive to the venue.

"I thought Sefina was joining us?" I ask Grace as we get out of the car.

"She'll be here shortly. She said there was something she needed to do, but she wouldn't give me details."

We take the elevator up to the bridal suite, where we find a spread of finger foods and drinks. The glass doors leading to the balcony are wide open, allowing the breeze from the water to blow into the room. The beachfront resort allows us an unobstructed view of the sea and is unlike anything I've ever laid eyes on. The longer I'm here, the easier it is to understand why Grace calls Hawaii home.

While we're enjoying the snacks, Sefina arrives with the stylist right behind her.

Before the chaos of getting ready ensues, Sefina pulls up a playlist of entrancing music. It fills the room with a sense of peace. With a renewed calmness. Everyone is able to enjoy this time without the usual pre-wedding nerves.

Grace has opted for simple hairstyles and minimal make-up, so although there are a lot of us, nothing is rushed.

The afternoon sun is beginning to wane, which is our cue to get dressed. I've chosen a chiffon sleeveless maxi dress that's pale blue. Gil will be wearing a linen shirt the same color as my dress. Sefina is wearing a more traditional Hawaiian-style dress. It's a floral purple ombre. Liko will be wearing a matching shirt. The bridesmaids are all wearing strapless chiffon dresses that are a soft pink.

Grace is the last to get dressed. Between the glow of pregnancy and her excitement of being a bride, she's radiant.

"It looks like we planned just right," Grace says and rubs her hand over the tiny baby bump she has. "It fits perfectly."

My eyes prick with tears when I look at my daughter. "My baby girl is all grown up."

"Don't make me cry, mom." Grace smiles.

"I have a gift for you." I reach into my bag, grab the little box, and hand it to her.

She tears it open and lifts the lid off. Inside is a delicate pearl necklace with a wedding day poem. Grace reads the poem aloud but quickly becomes too emotional to finish. Ivy steps in and reads it for her.

"Thank you, Mom. Can you put it on?" She turns around and carefully moves her hair out of the way so I can fasten the string of pearls around her neck.

"That's your something new," Frannie says. "Here's your something old." She hands her sister her favorite pair of pearl earrings. The girls exchange hugs.

"I have your something borrowed," Ivy adds and hands Grace a diamond bracelet. "Your brother bought it for me for our wedding."

"It's beautiful. Thank you so much." Grace reaches for a tissue and dabs at her eyes. "I didn't want to start crying already."

"I have your something blue." Sefina hands Grace what looks to be an old piece of light blue lace. "This has been in our family for five generations. If I have your permission, I can weave it into your bouquet."

"I'd be honored," Grace responds as another tear escapes. "Thank you all for making today so special for me. I love you all so much."

Sefina carefully weaves the delicate lace into Grace's bouquet. It's a beautiful addition to the pale pink and ivory roses. When she's finished, she hands the bouquet to Grace.

"It's time for you to go," Sefina says. "Makoa's cousins are waiting for you downstairs."

I kiss my daughter goodbye, knowing the next time I see her, she'll be walking down the aisle to say her wedding vows.

60

Gilbert

E veryone is seated. We're waiting for Grace and Makoa to arrive. They're doing a traditional ceremony with a few twists. Grace is being brought, by canoe, to meet Makoa at a secluded beach not far from the venue. She and Makoa will walk over to the area I'm waiting at so I can walk Grace down the aisle.

It isn't long before I see them come into view. My little girl is beaming. Makoa kisses her cheek and then walks away, heading to the venue, leaving Grace and me alone.

"Gracie girl," I fumble with my words. "You look beautiful."

The girls in the wedding party join us and exchange last-minute hugs and kisses with Grace before the music plays. The bridesmaids make their procession down the aisle to the traditional Hawaiin song, "Ke Kali Nei Au." Francesca is the maid of honor and the last one to go. Once the girls are in place, a man stands up and blows into the Pu, announcing Grace's pending arrival.

"Are you ready, dad?"

It takes a few seconds for me to find my words. The gravity of this moment is not lost on me. "Yes, I'm ready." And as hard as it is, I mean those words.

With my daughter's arm locked in mine, we make our way down the aisle to Israel Kamakawaio'ole's "Somewhere over the Rainbow."

I've had the privilege of raising this beautiful young woman, and now it's time to give her to Makoa, who's waiting for us.

When we get to the end of the aisle, Makoa reaches out to shake my hand. Then I place Grace's hand in his. "I'm entrusting my daughter to you, knowing you'll treasure her as much as I do."

"You have my word that I'll love and protect her with all I have, sir."

I nod and take my seat next to Liz.

"I'm proud of you," Liz whispers in my ear. "You did well."

If I try to speak, I'm going to cry. Instead, I take my wife's hand and turn my attention to the bride and groom.

The ceremony is beautiful. Grace and Makoa exchange lei's as the officiant explains the tradition is symbolic of the couple weaving their lives together. After a few words, Grace and Makoa say their vows. Neither makes it through without being overcome with emotions. The officiant then does a traditional Hawaiin ring blessing, something only done at beach weddings.

For me, the most moving part of the ceremony is the Pili ā nai kealoha which means love that binds. While "On this Day" by David Pomeranz plays, the officiant binds their hands together with a maile lei. While he wraps the vine, he explains the significance of marriage being a sign of enduring devotion and respect for one another.

After the ceremony, we spend the rest of the evening celebrating. This time Liz and I are there for the Luau. There's traditional Hawaiian music and hula dancing to open the reception. After they're done, a DJ takes their place, playing modern songs. The meal, an offering of the best foods the island has to offer, is mouthwateringly delicious.

61

Elizabeth

Gil is very quiet through the wedding ceremony. I catch him wiping at his eyes several times. Showing his emotions, especially in public, is not comfortable for him. So, I don't say anything. Instead, I hold his hand, offering him my love and quiet support.

We celebrate at a beachfront reception. In addition to the Hawaiian traditions, the newlyweds also include some of Grace's Italian heritage. A small wedding favor for each guest is arranged on the tables, Bomboniere, candied almonds. Each bag contains a little poem explaining the meaning of the treat—endurance and sweetness for the couple's new life together. The bags have an odd number of almonds because an odd number can't be divided into two, as the new couple is now one. Makao also cuts his tie into pieces that are placed on a tray. As they make their rounds greeting their guests, they collect money for pieces of the tie.

Once again, we're treated to a delicious offering of island foods. Sefina has promised to send me recipes so I can attempt to recreate the dishes we love the most.

After the meal, Grace and Makoa have their first dance to Caleb and Kelsey's beautiful rendition of "From this Moment on/You're Still the One." By the time the song is over, there isn't a dry eye. The DJ opens the dance floor to everyone, and the party begins. I assume I'll be sitting watching most of the evening, but Gil surprises me by grabbing my hand and leading me to the dance floor, where we dance the rest of the night.

Twenty-seven years and this man still surprises me.

As the reception begins to wind down, the DJ calls for all the single ladies to join Grace so she can throw her bouquet. Grace takes a quick look over her shoulder before tossing it behind her. Ke'ala catches the flowers.

"I'm next," she says and smiles proudly.

"Not for many years," Liko, who's standing next to us, says.

"I wouldn't count on that," Gil jokes.

The men share a look and then start laughing.

After the new couple says their goodbyes, Gil and I, along with Sefina and Liko, walk them down to the water where their canoe is waiting.

"Thank you for the beautiful wedding," Grace says. "It was more than I ever dreamed of."

"Take good care of my little girl," Gil addresses Makoa, who wraps his arm around Grace.

"Grace is my moon and stars—she's my life." He gazes adoringly at his new wife. "I will never let harm come to her or our little one." He caresses her tummy.

Gil swipes at a stray tear.

"Are you crying, daddy?" Grace asks.

"No. I must've got a piece of sand in my eye." He makes a show of rubbing his eye to remove the non-existent piece of sand.

We say our goodbyes and watch as Makoa helps Grace into the canoe. The two of them sail off into the night to begin their honeymoon.

Sefina and Liko return to the reception while Gil and I take a short walk along the sand.

"When we come for our anniversary trip, we should renew our vows by the beach," I suggest. "It's a very romantic setting."

"We'll have to look into that."

We walk hand-in-hand back to the reception, where the wedding guests are still dancing. A slow song plays, and Gil leads me to the dance floor again. As the music comes to an end, Gil whispers, "Let's make our exit. I'd like to be alone with my wife."

"I like the sound of that."

We make quick work of saying goodnight and return to our bungalow.

62

Elizabeth

Last night was a late night, so I'm not surprised when I wake and find it's close to two p.m. I reach over to wake Gil but find his spot on the bed empty. It's our last full day on the island, so I'm hoping we can go out and do something fun.

Grabbing my robe, I search for him, but he's nowhere to be found. Instead, I find a box wrapped in a red bow on the table in the sitting room.

When I get closer, I see there's a card attached to the bow. Opening it, I read the note.

Elizabeth, I've created a new box, especially for us. This one is entitled Wedding Vow Renewal. Inside you will find a few items for our private ceremony. I'll meet you on the beach in front of our bungalow at six forty-five p.m. Until then ~Gilbert P.S. Text me when you wake up.

Before I open the box, I send the text.

(Liz) Good afternoon. Sorry I slept so late. I just read your note. I can't wait. BTW, where are you?

(Gil) Good afternoon, sleeping beauty. Lunch will be delivered shortly. Take the rest of the afternoon for yourself.

(Liz) Okay, but where are you?

(Gil) I'm on the island. I'll see you this evening.

I make quick work of removing the bow and opening the box. Inside is a lei and a coordinating bouquet of colorful island flowers in shades of oranges and yellows. I'm still admiring the fragrant flowers when there's a knock on my door.

When I answer it, a woman holds a silver tray with a covered plate on it.

"I'm guessing this is my lunch."

"It is," the woman replies. "I hope you enjoy it."

I take the tray and bring it into the kitchenette. When I remove the cloche, I find an ahi poke bowl and a side of fresh fruit. Ahi Poke made my top five favorite foods I've discovered on the island.

After I have a leisurely lunch, I go through my outfits for what I'm going to wear tonight. I settle on a soft pink flowy sundress and a pair of sandals. There're still a few hours until I'm supposed to meet Gil. I debate on whether I should start packing or not. Gil said to take the afternoon for me, so I decide to spend the rest of the day on the lanai reading a book and soaking up the sunshine.

The day has flown by, another thing I'm going to miss when we go home—leisurely afternoons on the beach. Maybe we can retire here? I head back inside to shower and start getting ready for tonight.

I'm putting on my robe when there's another knock on the door. When I open it, there's a woman with a large bag in her hand.

"Mrs. Benton?" the woman asks.

"Yes."

"My name is Isla. I'm here to do your hair and make-up for tonight."

"I wasn't expecting this. Please come in."

Isla and I hit it off immediately. She's a transplant from New York City.

"I was sick of the constant hustle and bustle," she explains. "So, one day, I packed up and came to Hawaii. I'd never been here before. I had no house and no job. My family thought I was nuts."

"I think it was brave."

"Looking back, it was a crazy move. But I don't regret it. I love my life here."

"I can see why. I'm going to miss it when we go home."

"Are you ready to see your hair?" Isla asks.

I nod, and she hands me a mirror.

Isla created magic. There's a loose French braid on one side that connects with the rest of my hair in the back, hanging in long, loose curls. She's put tiny orange rosebuds in the updo.

"It's gorgeous."

Make-up is next. We decide on simple and understated. I love the look she's created.

"You're beautiful, Liz." Isla hugs me. "I hope you and your husband have a wonderful evening."

It's time to get dressed. I only have about a half-hour before I'm supposed to meet Gil on the beach.

I pull the door open and am startled to see Gil standing on the other side. He's wearing a Hawaiian shirt that matches the colors in my bouquet and a pair of white linen pants. Around his neck is a ti leaf lei.

"You look radiant, Lizzie." He offers me his hand. "Come with me."

He leads me down to our private piece of beach where there are tiki torches in the sand. They flicker in the light breeze. The sun is just beginning to set, casting hues of pinks and oranges as if the sky coordinates with our colors.

We slip off our shoes and stand at the water's edge, letting the soft waves lap at our feet.

"Elizabeth, I thought after all the years we've been together, nothing could break us. I became complacent with my responsibilities as your husband. My love never wavered, but I didn't convey my feelings as I should've." Gil takes my hand. "From this day forward, I promise to never take you or our marriage for granted. I vow to be the man you need me to be. I will not let a day go by that I don't show you how much I love you. I will care for you and honor you for as long as we both shall live."

I blink through my tears as I listen to my husband renew his vows to me.

"Gilbert, when I thought I lost you, my world went black. It felt as though a piece of me died. I don't ever want to feel that kind of loss again. I'm also guilty of letting life get in the way and come before us. I promise not to allow that ever again. I promise to put you first every day. I will care for you and honor you, as my husband, for as long as we both live."

Gil lets go of my hand and then pulls something out of his pocket. He opens up a small black box. Inside is a beautiful diamond band.

"Will you be my wife, again?"

"A million times, yes."

Gil slides the ring on my finger above my diamond. They glisten in the moonlight. Pulling me close, he wraps me in his strong arms and kisses me.

A few weeks ago, I didn't think I'd ever get to experience Gil's arms around me or the way he makes me feel like the only woman in the room. We aren't perfect, that's obvious, but we don't need to be. All we need is to be ourselves, two imperfect people who have chosen to take this journey of real life romance together.

The End

Dear Reader

Thank you for reading Real Life Romance. I hope you've enjoyed Gilbert and Elizabeth's story. If you did (or even if you didn't), can you please take a moment to leave me a review. It doesn't have to be long—unless you want it to be. Each and every review is important to me and I thank you for them.

I fell in love with Gilbert's character which didn't start off the way you read him. Gil wanted to tell his story on his terms and that included highlighting his high functioning autism. He is hoping to shed some light on autism and that people with it can lead a very normal life. If you know someone with autism or you are looking to learn more, check out the site www.autism-speaks.org . It's a great resource and one that's helped me along the way as I raised a child with high functioning autism.

Did RealLifeRomance.org pique your interest? Check out the actual website where you can find not only bookish merchandise, but also all the fun date ideas from the book and more!

Happy Reading
~Tara

Coming Soon

Viktor is returning to her home country with a broken heart. He attempts to heal the hole left by doing what he does best—ridding the world of crime. When he disappears for too long, Maxim sets out to find him and bring him back. He has a personal job for Viktor, one that brings more complications than he was prepared for. Viktor's story will be an age gap romance that you don't want to miss.

Also By

Fire and Ice World (Alex and Natalie)

Submitting to Him (Book One)
Fighting with Him (Book Two)
Living for Him (Book Three)

Acknowledgments

First, I want to thank my husband. You are my real life romance, my inspiration, my support on days I want to give up. I love you forever and a day.

To my mom- I finally wrote a book you'll read. Thank you for being my beta reader and proofreader. I hope you enjoy it.

Aunt Chi Chi- Thank you for helping with the editing!

To my kids- The four of you have taught me how the "sibling code" works and are the inspiration behind Gilbert and Elizabeth's family. Without each of you, I wouldn't be able to do any of this. I love you guys.

To the real-life Chef Marc- I hope you like your cameo appearance.

A huge thank you to Erica Alexander for helping with my blurb and tagline!

To my BETA readers- thank you for being willing to read multiple drafts and for your honest feedback. I am so grateful for each of you.

About Author

Tara Conrad is a happily collared submissive and is married to her husband/Dominant, George. Together they have four young adult children. When Tara isn't writing, you can find her reading or hanging out with her husband. Tara embarked on this author journey late in life but is loving every second of this ride.

You can keep in touch with her and see what she's up to next by following her on social media:

Discover more books by Tara at www.taraconradauthor.com

You can also follow her on social media:

Facebook: @TaraConradAuthor

Goodreads @t.l.conrad

Instagram: @taraconradauthor

Twitter: @TLConrad1

TikTok @TaraConradauthor

Bookbub: @TaraConradAuthor

Newsletter: https://mailchi.mp/df5501ebffe0/newsletter-sign-up

Made in the USA
Middletown, DE
27 March 2022

63150898R00137